A WWII Historical Fiction Novel

THE
SEAMSTRESS
OF
AUSCHWITZ

PAPER FOREST PRESS

C. K. McADAM

In memory of the six million.

"Where they have burned books, they will end in burning human beings."

~ Heinrich Heine, German-Jewish Poet (1823)

PROLOGUE
2019

I've been dying for fifteen years. Two pacemakers and four resuscitations later, here I am on my 100th birthday surrounded by my son, daughter-in-law, grandchildren, and great-grandchildren in an assisted living home. All of them wear at least one article of clothing I designed, sewed, and fashioned for them over the past few years.

The last time I sat in front of my sewing machine was only a month ago. I needed help with threading the needle because of my trembling hands, but sewing means I'm alive. When I inevitably had to accept that I was no longer able to get to and use my machine, I knew; it was the beginning of the end.

I cough, and a warm hand rests over mine. I don't know whose. Perhaps my son's, but I don't look. Instead, I search the faces of the people gathered around the foot of my bed.

My family.

I don't care for my birthday. I never did, but especially at my age, is there a point in celebrating? Yet, as I take in their faces on the day of my last, the faces of all the people who care for me, I privately admit that this birthday is indeed very special.

There aren't many who reach the age of 100.

Even the local paper came to interview the centenarian. Though of course, the reporter had been most interested in what happened to me during the war. I gave the journalist the general gist of my story, but after thirty minutes, I asked him to leave so I could spend time with my family. Thankfully, he was understanding and left without complaint.

My family already knows my story. Every detail. I wrote it all down for my son Paul, so he could pass it on to his children and they to their own. My loved ones who perished shouldn't be forgotten. Their memory must be the blessing birthed from a nightmare. I made Paul and my grandchildren promise to keep their late relatives alive through the tales of their trials.

And mine.

As I close my eyes, those very memories flood my mind, stirred up by the interview. The fading footsteps of the journalist still echo in my ears an hour later.

The voices around me grow distant and muted. I surrender to the muffled peace and let the familiar faces of the past engulf me. Just for a moment.

CHAPTER 1

1932

"Don't let Sara do it!" Helene pushed me out of her way to get to one of the sewing machines first.

"Ouch." I rubbed my arm and threw her a withering look, but I knew better than to challenge her. Helene was eighteen months older, almost a head taller, and much stronger than me. I stepped back and let my sister sit down on the chair in front of the shiny black machine with the gold lettering. After all, it was hers.

I weaved my way to the chaise lounge and plopped down, unfazed by the surrounding chaos. I leaned back, fidgeting with the green velvet, and tried to stifle a loud sigh. The buzzing energy in our sitting room had intensified over the last few hours. Alice, my oldest sister, was getting married tomorrow, and we tried to make last-minute alterations to her dress. All under the direction of both her and my mother, after whom I'd been named.

The Schönflieses were a family of tailors and seamstresses, living above my father's shop, which he'd inherited from his father, who'd also been a tailor. Grandfather had fought in the Great War but died shortly after of injuries he'd sustained in France. He'd received a medal for his bravery, which my father proudly had on display in a glass cabinet in his shop.

My father's severe stutter had disqualified him from serving in the Kaiser's army. My mother called it a blessing.

Father was the tailor in our small town of Salzhausen, talented and with once high aspirations. My mother was a seamstress in her own right and handled all our family's sewing needs. She'd taught my sisters and me well—except for my youngest sister, Clara, whose arrival six years ago had been a surprise. But it was my father who'd taught us more than just mending, darning, and repairing articles of clothing.

Together with Alice, he'd designed her wedding dress. Months ago, they'd hunched over her gown in the workroom at the back of the shop for endless hours. Fashion magazines Alice loved to read and had inspired her dress had been strewn about. Piles of white lace had covered half the worktable. My father had been softly singing folk songs while cutting and sewing and only occasionally letting his hands rest to instruct Alice to hand him a pair of scissors or undo stitches. I'd been surprised at my father's fervor for designing and making her dress, but he loved to create, not just mend and repair.

The rhythmic humming of the sewing machine and Helene muttering under her breath while carefully yielding lace brought me back to the tension thickening the air. But since I was banned from helping with the last-minute alterations my mother deemed necessary for Alice's dress, I grabbed my book from the table. I searched for the page I'd been reading, and her annoying mumbling faded away as the words took me elsewhere.

I only looked up when the whir of the sewing machine stopped, and the room had fallen into hushed silence. All traces of urgency had vanished, replaced by dulled yet distinct clops echoing from the street below.

I threw my book carelessly back onto the table and flew to the window. My little sister Clara was next to me in an instant, and I pulled the curtain aside so we could have a full view of the street below. Helene joined us. Her brows were furrowed, and she pushed out her lower jaw, a sign of anger or defiance.

The rhythmic thumps of boots on cobblestones drowned out our ragged breaths. The brown shirts, many of them not older than my brother Georg, marched down our street. It was an almost daily occurrence. Their puffed-out chests and newly shined footwear made them look ridiculous, and I sneered at them. Helene joined me.

Mother huffed from behind us. "Get away from window, girls." Her Polish accent was more pronounced than usual. "I don't want them see us gawking." Helene and I withdrew, pulling Clara with us. Mother adjusted the curtains. "We don't have time idling. Helene, finish sleeves. Alice needs to try dress one last time. Sara and Clara, you coming with me to kitchen."

I wanted to protest and return to my book, but there were a million things left to do before the wedding, and Mother wouldn't tolerate me arguing my way out of it.

Reluctantly, I followed her and Clara out of the room.

In the kitchen, my Polish grandmother Ada stood by the stove, stirring a pot of what I suspected contained her famed *rosol*, a Polish chicken noodle soup. *Bobe*, as we called her, had passed on the recipe to my mother. And Mother cooked it at least once a week. It was considered a remedy for all sorts of ailments in our home. I never grew tired of it.

I went over to Bobe and peered into the pot. She smiled and began speaking in Yiddish. I understood most of it thanks to the summers I'd spent in Poland at my grandparents' house, but I wasn't able to speak it well. I smiled back and rested my head on her shoulder.

Bobe was my favorite grandmother. She was a great storyteller, like many people in Chelm where she'd lived all her life, and she was kind. My father's mother, Oma Ruth, on the other hand, was stern, and I never felt at ease around her. I saw her more often than Bobe because she lived just down the street from us.

My great-grandfather had been a wealthy merchant, and she'd enjoyed a privileged upbringing with piano lessons and fur coats. Why she'd married my grandfather, a tailor, was a mystery that had not been shared with us children. Every time she spent time with us, she expected my sisters and me to act and look 'perfect.' Something I wasn't. Only Alice could ever please her.

Bobe, on the other hand, loved us all despite our imperfections and, at times, ill behavior.

She pulled me over to the table where my mother and Clara already sat, peeling a mountain of potatoes. My grandmother started humming a Yiddish folk song. Mother joined in. I too quickly fell into a rhythm of peeling spuds until the door flew open, and my Aunt Irene's jolly face appeared.

My father's sister was a teacher in Altstädt, the neighboring town. She'd never married, but Aunt Irene spoiled us as if we were her own children and spent every Shabbat and holiday with us.

Mother handed her an apron, and she sat down to peel potatoes with us.

After a few minutes, she interrupted the singing. "I saw a Minerva in the paper." My aunt put the knife on the table and wiped her hands on the apron. She pulled a folded newspaper from her purse and held it out to me with a nod.

"Let me see." Excited, my mother swiped the newspaper from Aunt Irene and proceeded to the ad page.

"It's on the very bottom." Aunt Irene's voice now matched my mother's. She turned to me and smiled. "It's perfect for you." I looked at her, wide-eyed, and erupted into a smile of excitement myself.

My mother read the ad and nodded approvingly. It was a rite of passage in our family to get your own sewing machine for your fourteenth birthday, and I would turn fourteen in November, only a few months away. I had asked for a Minerva.

Named for the Roman goddess of commerce, weaving, crafts, and wisdom, the shining black machine with gold lettering would be honored and respected and serve me in creating beautiful articles of fashion.

It would be the first valuable object I would ever own. Well, except for the sterling silver necklace I always wore, given by my parents at my bat mitzvah.

I turned to Mother. "May I see?" She handed me the newspaper, and my eyes fell immediately on the black-and-white image at the bottom of the page. It was an older model. Used. Not the brand-new one I had seen in my sister's fashion magazines. But my brother and Alice had also received a used sewing machine on their birthdays.

Our family wasn't rich. Father's tailor shop supported us, but any extravagance was out of the question.

Georg had taken his sewing machine with him to America. Alice would soon take hers to her new home with her husband. It was a gift that would bring us into adulthood and help us earn a living. My Minerva would be with me for the rest of my life; a comforting thought.

"It's perfect." I smiled and touched the image on the page. Only a few more months.

"Then it's settled. I inquire after wedding," Mother said, with a confirming nod in my direction.

We turned our attention back to the potatoes. We had a wedding meal to prepare.

"Get up! Get up!" Clara shook me awake. I tried to bat her away like a fly, but my efforts were in vain. She jumped on the bed, which creaked precariously. I tried to kick her off—there was a thump, followed by a yelp.

I opened my eyes. She lay on the floor, about to cry. "I'm getting up. Stop pestering me, *la nuisance*."

Clara was already dressed in a beautiful floral dress with a bright white starched collar my father had made for her. Her blond hair had been curled and was held back on one side by a giant bow. She looked like a doll.

My own dress hung over a chair in the corner of the room I shared with Clara and Helene. I'd been looking forward to wearing it. Alice had lent me a stack of her magazines and let me choose a style. She'd made my dress, as well as Helene's, who didn't really care about dresses and preferred to wear trousers, to the disapproval of our mother.

I quickly got dressed and brushed my hair, which I preferred hanging loosely down my back, then headed downstairs. I dodged the kitchen, looking for Father. I hadn't yet told him about the sewing machine Aunt Irene had found in the paper. Even on a day like this, I knew I would find him in his workshop.

As a young man, he had aspired to move to Berlin to apprentice and open the finest suit emporium in the capital. He'd eventually made it to Berlin the year before the Great War.

During his first week there, he met my mother on the steps of the synagogue on Shabbat. He said it was love at first sight after she'd noticed and praised his fine suit. My mother, who had just arrived from Poland, together with a cousin, didn't mind Father's stutter and took a liking to him.

After only a few months in Berlin, the war broke out. My father's mother, grandmother Ruth, insisted her son come home and take over his father's tailor shop since he'd been drafted to the trenches in France. That same day, my father proposed to my mother, and she agreed to come with him to Salzhausen.

They were married and had us, one boy and four girls. We grew up above Father's shop and learned his trade. As soon as my brother Georg was old enough, our father sent him to a cousin in America, so he could pursue Father's dream of a suit emporium there.

I entered the workshop. My father was leaning over his worktable, already dressed in his finest. In front of him was an unfinished suit with chalk marks dotting the fabric. A packet of needles and a pair of scissors lay to the side. He smiled when I came in.

"Your sister m-m-m-made you a b-b-beautiful d-d-d-d-dress." He looked at me approvingly. He struggled with his speech more than usual. Maybe it was Alice's wedding. The glasses on his nose meant he'd been working. Mother had begged him not to do so on the day of his daughter's wedding, but he always worked—except on Shabbat and the holidays.

"Did Mother show you the ad for the Minerva?" I asked.

"She d-d-did. A f-f-f-fine machine. It will s-s-serve you well." He took his glasses off and gave me a scrutinizing look. "You will f-f-finish this school year, then you will a-a-app-pp ..." He paused and sucked in a deep breath to focus his speech. "A-a-a-pp-pp-pprentice with me." He breathed out slowly.

It wasn't a question and what he said wasn't unexpected, either. Georg and Alice had done the same before me.

"Unless it's n-n-not what you want," he added, searching my face. I stopped kneading my hands. Oh, I had a choice? But what else would I do? Stay in school like Helene, despite her exceptional talent for sewing? There was nothing else I wanted to do or had planned. "You think on that," he said, interrupting my thoughts. I nodded. "N-n-now, we need to close up. Mother and Alice will not be h-h-happy if they f-f-find us down here today."

―――――

My sister's face was veiled, and I wondered how she was able to see, let alone walk so confidently to the chuppah where her groom waited for her.

Alice was barely eighteen, but her maturity belied her age. Still too young to marry, in my opinion. I would never get married that young. Or ever. I still couldn't believe Father had agreed to the marriage, but Mother had barely been eighteen when they'd married.

The groom, Hershel Wolf, came from a respectable family in Altstädt, but as a boy, he'd been arrogant and had taunted Alice and the other girls in his school. He'd begun acting kindly and respectfully toward our family since he'd started courting Alice, but I couldn't understand what my sister saw in him. He wasn't particularly handsome, and his hair had already begun to thin.

Alice circled around Hershel, her beautiful dress swishing. I glanced at Mother, who was weeping silently into her kerchief. Next to her, Helene was fidgeting with her dress. She muttered something under her breath that sounded like "wretched skirts." I chuckled, and Oma Ruth shot me a stern and disapproving glance. A hand rested on my shoulder, and I turned around. Bobe winked at me, and I quickly stifled another chuckle. I straightened my shoulders and turned my attention back to Alice and Hershel.

The rabbi finished his blessing and offered a cup of wine to the couple. Hershel presented a plain gold ring and slipped it on Alice's right ring finger. Then the rabbi and my father took turns reading the seven blessings. My father struggled, but he was too proud to let anyone read for him. It was his role, and he took it seriously. With the readings complete, Father held the cup of wine to Hershel's lips, and Alice's mother-in-law to hers.

Hershel stepped on a kerchief covering a glass, crushing it with his right foot, and my sister was a married woman. Mother wept, Helene looked annoyed—and a realization dropped into my belly like a rock in a pond. Our family was forever changed. I didn't like Hershel, and Alice would no longer be at home.

I swallowed hard and suppressed the desire to cry along with my mother.

———

The wedding feast at our town's hall, which Father had rented for the festivities, was packed with family and friends of the bride and groom. After the wedding meal, the dancing began. I don't know if it was the music or Aunt Irene, but I surprisingly enjoyed that part of the celebration. The frantic music, the faster and faster dancing, and the unison of the crowd put me in a trance.

For a while, I forgot all my anger about Alice getting married—until brownshirts stormed the hall, right as Hershel and Alice were lifted into the air on their chairs.

A hushed silence fell as the six stormtroopers strode toward the circle of men who had lowered the bride and groom back to the floor. On their way through throngs of wedding guests, which parted like the Red Sea, they still pushed people and chairs alike out of their way. I anxiously searched the guests for Father's face and found him standing close to Alice and Hershel.

The rabbi stepped in front of the intruders and held up his hands. "We don't want any trouble."

The tallest of the brownshirts, a rather lanky man, responded by swiping him square across the face. "Out of my way, Jew," he barked and pushed past the rabbi, who was holding his bleeding nose.

I grabbed my aunt's hand. She squeezed mine as if to assure me everything would be fine.

They reached my father, and without a word, they grabbed both his arms and dragged him out of the hall. He didn't protest nor resist, neither did any of the wedding guests, though a heartbroken rasp escaped Mother.

The fear clawing at my belly was written across everyone's face. My mother looked from one man to another, her eyes pleading with them, but their faces were either blank or cast to the ground. No one was helping.

Alice cried on Hershel's shoulder; the festivities were over.

The guests left soon after.

Father didn't come home until the next morning. No one had gotten any sleep. When he came through the door just after the sun began to rise, illuminating our sitting room—and his face—we gasped. He was swollen and bloodied. One sleeve from his suit was missing, and his dress shirt was tattered. We ran to his side, but he had no words for us as he fell heavily onto a chair.

"Get bowl with warm water and clean cloth," my mother urged me. "Helene, run to Alice and tell her Father is home."

When I returned with the bowl, we stood around him, watching Mother dab and clean his face. He winced a few times. No one spoke. We waited patiently for him to say something, but he never did. Maybe to Mother later, but never to us children. Helene tried. After returning home with both Alice and Hershel in tow, she bombarded him with questions, but he only held up his hand to stop her inquisition.

But Helene was relentless. "We need to go to Palestine! Now! We can't wait any longer, Father. It's getting worse and worse."

Palestine. A faraway land. One of my Polish cousins had immigrated there. From what we understood from his occasional letters, life was tough and conditions harsh, and we spoke very little Hebrew. What would we do there? And where would we get all the money needed for everyone to travel there?

"We can't go to Palestine." Not only was our father's tone final as he pushed himself out of the chair, but he also hadn't stuttered.

For a moment, we all stared at him in disbelief. Mother cleared her throat and begged him to sit back down and rest, but he wouldn't listen. And we all knew where he was heading.

CHAPTER 2
1933

The bleak winter sun barely provided enough light in our dining room, but no one turned on the light. We'd pulled up chairs close to the side table on which our radio stood. Father and Mother had refused to put it in the sitting room, so we rarely used it, but it was important today that we listened.

Clara was the only one who didn't pay full attention. She had her toy tea set spread out across the dining room table. Her expression was somber as if someone had just scolded her.

My breathing was shallow, and I tried to understand the stream of shouts. The new chancellor's voice was rattling on with fervor. Hitler spoke of racial unity and the great country Germany would become again. The nationalists and national socialists considered Jews a different race, an inferior race, and Hitler made it clear we wouldn't be a part of the new Germany he envisioned.

No one spoke when his speech finished.

Helene and I looked at Mother and Father imploringly, but they ignored our silent questions. Instead, they put the chairs back around the table, and I helped Clara gather up her tea set.

"What was the man screaming about?" she asked, snapping the leaden silence. Her usual tiny voice resonated surprisingly loud. Our mother and father stopped arranging the chairs.

Father gently placed a hand on her blond head. "Nothing you need to worry a-a-about."

She peered at him with her big, round eyes and gave an obedient nod.

To deflect more, I added, "Let's continue this tea party in our room. I'm sure Bear would like a cup of tea."

Clara broke into a smile. It wasn't every day that one of her big sisters offered to play with her.

———

It was a crisp morning, the first of April, when Clara, Helene, and I stepped outside to make our way to school. I looked up at the dreary sky, void of any promises of spring. Helene hissed at me and pulled at my sleeve. I turned to her to give her a push, but my eyes fell onto our shop—and why she'd wanted my attention.

In front of Father's shop stood a boy from my class who, dressed in the uniform of the Hitler Youth, held up a sign warning Germans not to buy from Jews. A big white star of David had been painted across the entire store window front, standing in stark contrast to the black swastika on the boy's blood-red and white armband.

My face fell. I looked at Helene and Clara, who stared at the boy in front of our shop. Helene's facial expression changed from shock to anger, but all that coursed through me was heated shame.

I looked around the neighborhood. A couple on the other side of the street hastened by but didn't look up.

The boy, his face misleadingly friendly, ignored our presence completely. Had he seen us standing there, gaping at him? Would I see him at school today? And if so, would he harass me directly there?

Helene hissed that we should leave and pulled Clara and me with her down the sidewalk. On the next street corner, she stopped and looked at me, her brows furrowed. "If Germans are forbidden to come to our shop, how will Father get any business?" For the first time in my life, Helene sounded afraid.

Clara sensed something was wrong and started crying, Helene's fear was contagious even without the full context. Fear crept up in me, too, and I shuddered involuntarily.

"Maybe we should go home," I murmured.

Helene simply nodded. It was rare that she listened to me, but it wasn't a moment of sisterly triumph.

We walked the few meters back home, pretending the boy in front of our shop was indeed a statue.

———

I lifted my foot off the paddle, and my Minerva stopped whirring. Closing my eyes, I focused on the warm May air coming in from the open window brushing my face. I leaned back in my chair and stretched my achy back before opening my eyes and watching the flecks of sunlight dance across my sewing machine.

I'd been sewing for days. There was nothing else to do. Mother and Father had taken us out of school at the end of April. The bullying had increased, and some of the teachers had begun to ostracize us and the other Jewish students. The government had restricted school attendance for all Jewish children and university students in the Reich, forcing us to be homeschooled.

I was angry at them—and at Hitler for spoiling my last weeks of school. I missed my friends. I missed the routine. But I had to accept that I would never go back.

With a sigh, I stood up and closed the window. The daylight would soon wane, so I turned my attention back to my Minerva and the hemline of the skirt I was sewing.

When Mother called that it was time for dinner, I'd finished my skirt and held it up to examine it. Satisfied with my work, I went to the dining room.

Shabbat was about to begin.

———

I loved Shabbat. It was my favorite time of the week. We were all together, and no one was working. Plus, Alice would be home. Although I'd gotten used to her living apart from us, her presence and Shabbat made me feel like I was back in my earlier childhood. Happier times when I'd still been in school, the Nazi regime had only been a small irritant, and my sisters and I had played with no worries in the world.

Father had already lit the Shabbat candles when I entered the dining room. No one had sat down yet. I searched for Alice; she stood next to the radio with our mother, talking quietly.

I rushed over to her and hugged her. She laughed. "You saw me only two days ago."

"Yes, but I used to see you every day," I retorted, not quite ready to let go of her until our father cleared his throat.

We all sat down, except Father, who would offer the prayer, as he always did. Only then did I notice Hershel. It was impossible to ignore his attendance once, to my annoyance, Father asked Hershel to say the Kiddush and pass around the cup.

Resting his hand on the challah bread, my father proceeded to bless it and gave each of us a piece. Mother filled our soup plates, and we ate quietly.

"Have you heard?" Aunt Irene, who always spent Shabbat with us as well, interrupted the clanking of spoons against porcelain. Father shot her a look that seemed to be a warning, but she didn't heed it. "They burnt all sorts of books last night. At the university campus. Can you believe it?"

"What books?" I blurted out.

"Who is burning books?" Clara asked, her eyes wide.

Father shot his sister another warning look, but my aunt continued to ignore him. "All kinds of books, I heard. German writers. Jewish writers. Any books they don't approve—"

"But *who* is burning them?" Helene interjected.

"Students and even professors." Aunt Irene looked down at her soup as if it held an explanation. She hadn't joined the family business but had studied at the university to become a teacher. My aunt loved books and always shared them with us girls. The book burnings must have horrified her: they horrified me! I'd come to love books as much as she did, her passion for them contagious.

I glanced at the built-in bookshelf in our dining room. The brown and red covers of the classics, from Goethe to Schiller to Heine, Mendelsohn, Lessing, and Rilke stood neatly next to each other. As children, we'd not been allowed to touch them, but once we turned twelve, my father would take one of them off the shelf and command us to read it right there at the table. The classics were never allowed to leave the dining room.

The books Aunt Irene brought us were fairy tales, myths, and legends, which we devoured as children.

Father and Mother had ignored the news Irene shared and continued spooning their soup silently.

I jumped when my aunt's spoon clattered into her bowl, and she leaned back in her chair. She looked at all of us, her face pained. "Heinrich Heine said a hundred years ago that where they burn books, they'll also burn people."

We all stared.

What could one of the great German poets who'd been born a Jew have meant by that? I pushed away the mental image of a condemned witch burning at the stake. But another visual invaded my mind. People and buildings burning. People *in* buildings burning. In our people's long history, Christians had burnt Jews and Jewish synagogues, but this was the twentieth century, not the Middle Ages. I narrowed my eyes.

Helene hit the table with her fist. She opened her mouth to speak, but Father stood up and left the table before she could utter a word, and Mother shot her a warning look. Helene snapped her jaw shut and remained silent.

The heat was oppressive in Chelm. We always spend parts of our summer holidays with our grandparents in Poland, but it was the second time we visited my grandparents, Bobe and Zayde, without Alice. So, it was just Helene, Clara, and I making our way to the little swimming lake at the edge of town to cool off for the afternoon.

When we got to the lake, the local youth had already spread out along the banks, many splashing around in the water. Helene spotted her Zionist friends and headed in their direction without a care about Clara and me; she always abandoned us at the first opportunity.

I scanned the grassy bank to the left. There was an empty spot near where Helene stood talking enthusiastically to her friends, some of them appearing much older than her and me. I rolled my eyes and headed to the available spot, pulling Clara with me.

As I was setting my bag down, three boys my age appeared out of nowhere. "That's our spot," one of them said, looking determined.

Clara tried to pull me away, but I shook off her hand. "We were here first," I snapped defiantly in broken Polish. Who did they think they were? Clara took refuge behind me, away from the strangers and the confrontation.

"Is there a problem?" Two of Helene's friends had come over to see what was going on while Helene stood off to the side, brows furrowed and lower jaw pushed out.

"This is none of your business, Jew," another of the boys quipped, his hands balled into fists.

Helene finally stepped forward, but one of her friends put his hand on her shoulder to halt her and approached in her stead. He strode up to the boys, who seemed no more than two years younger than him. "If you don't want any trouble, I suggest you get out of here." Helene's friend was as calm as the lake's water on the hot summer afternoon.

The boy who'd spoken first stepped closer to him, but he got pulled back by his friends. "Dirty Jews," he hissed and spat on the ground.

The knots in my gut only eased when they turned tail and walked away, but I didn't feel like swimming anymore.

Neither did Clara. "Can we go home?" she whispered.

I simply nodded. With a glance at Helene, who remained rooted in place, I picked up the bag, and we left.

Chelm was not the first and only place where we had been called "dirty Jews." Since Hitler had become chancellor in January, not just the brownshirts harassed us. Even some people in our small town in Germany, whom we'd known all of our lives, called us names, avoided us, or grew tense and cold around us.

We tried to ignore it. My parents especially didn't want to talk about it. We were one of a few Jewish families in Salzhausen, and my father had been a respectable member of the community all his life, partially because he was the only tailor in town. But Chelm was twice the size of our town, with almost half its citizens being Jews who'd lived there for centuries. They'd been part of the local community for just as long, if not longer than the Schönflies had been at home.

Regardless, there'd always been prejudice and the occasional bullying, but that summer in Chelm was different. That summer, those who hated us no longer hid their animosity.

———

After dinner, Helene told Bobe and Zayde in broken Yiddish what had happened at the lake, and we were forbidden to go there for the remainder of our stay. We protested, but our pleas didn't change their minds.

Zayde left to sit on the bench in front of their little house to whittle in the dying evening light, and Helene took Clara up to the attic, where the three of us slept, to put her to bed.

Bobe turned to me and padded my cheek. "Bubala, don't worry. I tell you story. It is great story. I am surprised I have not told you story." Her soothing melodic Yiddish calmed me, despite only being able to grasp a portion of what she said.

I nestled in her arms, hoping I'd be able to understand the details of her story.

She told me about the chief rabbi of Chelm, who'd lived centuries ago. From clay, the rabbi had formed a golem which he used as a servant and a protector of the Jews of the city. On market days, the golem would stand ready, with an ax in hand, and defend the Jews of Chelm against any Christians who would harass them. When the Christians threatened to destroy the golem in outrage, the rabbi returned him to a heap of clay, which had been moved to and stored in the attic of the synagogue.

"We should get the—what did you call it?"

"Golem," Bobe said.

"We should get the golem. Go to the synagogue. To the attic. We need him," I said half-jokingly.

"Not possible," Bobe explained that the attic had been locked and that since then, no one had dared to venture there. "Rabbi took key to grave."

That night in my bed in my grandparents' attic, I related the story in whispers to Helene, who said she'd heard the legend before, but she listened intently nevertheless.

"You know that this is all a fairy tale, right?" she said. "And I heard another version of that story. One where the golem went crazy and destroyed everything. Besides, I don't think the synagogue even has an attic. But we could check." I stared, mouth agape, and she grinned before continuing more seriously, "There is no golem that will save us, Sara. We can only save ourselves. We are the golem, don't you see?"

I fell back on my pillow and pondered Helene's words. Of course, only she would say such a thing. She wasn't afraid of confrontation and felt strongly about any perceived injustice. But she was right. We needed to defend ourselves and not be pushovers, to show the anti-Semites that we wouldn't take their abuse.

But what about the government and all the restrictions? All the open persecution? How far would it go?

"I've been thinking—" Helene interrupted my thoughts. "It's time to get out of here."

"What do you mean?" I sat up again, trying to make out her face in the dark.

"As soon as I'm eighteen, I'll undertake *Aliyah*."

"What do you mean?" I understood the definition, but not what Helene meant by it.

"I will go to Palestine," she said.

"What? You can't!"

"Ssshhhhhh," she hissed. "You're going to wake up Clara."

"Palestine? Alone? Father and Mother will never let you go."

"I said I'll go when I'm eighteen. They need to let me go then," she said defiantly. She was only a little over a year away from her eighteenth birthday. She would leave us all? Just like that? I would never. So far away. All by herself? "Well, goodnight. I'm sleeping now." Helene turned around with a huff.

I stared at her dark form. Would I lose another sister?

I dreamed of Palestine that night, but in my dreams, it was a strange, desolate place where giant golems made of clay roamed freely, swinging axes at any living thing.

When we arrived back home after two weeks with Bobe and Zayde, none of us shared with our parents what had happened at the lake.

Clara seemed to have forgotten, and Helene and I had sworn each other to secrecy.

In a few days, the apprenticeship with my father would officially begin. I had already been taught how to sew by hand and with a machine, but Father would also show me how to design, draft, and cut patterns, something Alice was especially good at. I'd also learn how to properly press and fit the garments I'd create. At least, I hoped I'd be taught all that. Father had noticeably less business, and I wondered how he would justify and manage using materials to teach me without being compensated.

To have fewer bodies in the workshop and make room for me, and to give Helene something to do, she was sent to Aunt Irene, who'd started teaching Jewish children in her home. I hoped Aunt Irene needing Helene's help would cross her plans to leave for Palestine, but I was keenly aware that our family, and life in Germany, were changing forever.

Never again would it be like when we were all young.

Though my sense of loss was somewhat pacified by Father's enthusiasm to teach me.

CHAPTER 3

1938

M y knees ached from having spent the last two hours on the hard floor playing with my little niece. The toddler looked up at me when I let out a groan while pushing up onto my feet and rubbing my sore knees. Alice's little girl, whom she'd named Ruth after our German grandmother who'd died last year, got up as well, hanging onto my skirt. I scooped her up and bounced her on my hip.

Alice came in and took her from me. "It's time for bed, little treasure." I relinquished my hold on Ruth, but she kept clinging to me. I was her favorite aunt, but she also hated bedtime. Alice finally managed to pull her off me.

After they left the room, I cleaned up the rag doll and its clothes, which I'd sewn from scraps of fabric, strewn around on the floor of Alice's and Hershel's small kitchen.

I noticed the waning light outside and hurried to the front door. With one arm in my coat, I bellowed a hasty goodbye in the direction of Alice's bedroom and slipped out the door. I swung on my bike and paddled down the alley, the cobblestone rattling the old bike and me in the process. When I finally left Altstädt behind where both

Alice and Hershel, as well as Aunt Irene and Helene lived, the sun already began to dip behind the far-off hills to the West.

I paddled even harder to make it home before the imposed curfew. I would visit Helene and Aunt Irene, who ran a small school for Jewish children in the back of her house, another day. While I missed Helene, I was grateful to know she was with Aunt Irene, who'd understood and even shared Helene's desire to go to Palestine but had convinced her that they were needed right where they were.

Helene had taken to teaching and never mentioned Palestine again.

Just as darkness fell, I arrived home sweaty and out of breath, despite the cold air. Father's shop lay dark and abandoned. The only light that fell onto the street came from the second and third floors. Father rarely went downstairs anymore. With almost no customers, the few orders he received and fulfilled were from friends and relatives and mostly done in our sitting room. Most of the time, he was mending clothes.

I wasn't sure if he still went to his workshop where he'd spent most of his life, or if he avoided it out of fear and for the lack of materials and customers. I never saw him there anymore, but I also was gone a lot of the time.

My apprenticeship ended up being nothing like how I'd envisioned it. Father pulled me occasionally aside to teach me a few new skills, but most of my knowledge came from Alice and her old fashion magazines. Whenever I visited her, she would pull out an old dress, blouse, or skirt, unravel it, and show me how to turn it into a fashionable article of clothing. Mother or Father would have never let us do that. Especially now. Such frivolity wouldn't be tolerated. Luckily, they didn't know what we were up to.

In return for taking me under her wing and teaching me more than just mending clothes, I helped Alice take care of Ruth. I ended up spending most of my days with Alice rather than at home. We became very close, closer than I anticipated possible following her marriage.

I pulled my bike inside and rested it against the wall of the dark hallway and made my way upstairs. Clara, who recently turned eleven, greeted me at the door with a grin. I looked at her perplexed. "What is it, *la nuisance*?"

"He was here. And you missed him ... because you're late," Clara said in a half-amused, half-irritated way.

"Who?"

"Solomon, of course."

"What did he want? ... Again." I rolled my eyes as I hung up my coat. Clara had no answer for me, just a smirk. I pushed past her to make my way to the kitchen where I'd find Mother and hopefully a bowl of her soup.

"You finally come home." My mother motioned for me to sit down at the table. I did so willingly. I was starving because I never ate at Alice's, even when she offered. They were struggling like so many others, and I refused to be a burden to her.

Mother placed a soup plate of rosol and a slice of bread in front of me and sat down across the table. "How's Alice? Little Ruth?"

"They are doing well," I said between blows and spoonfuls.

"Solomon came by for visit again today." She gave me an imploring look.

I sighed. "I don't know why he keeps coming. I told him I'm not interested."

"He's fine young man. From good family."

"Well, I don't like him, Mother. Please don't encourage him." I stood up and went to the sink to wash my dish. My mother sighed behind me.

Solomon Baumann had been in my class, and he'd always had a crush on me. But he wasn't my type. Not that I knew what my type was, but he certainly wasn't it. I sat back down, hoping she would drop the topic.

A loud crash echoed from downstairs. We startled, then froze, staring at each other. Clara, now in her nightgown, came running into the kitchen and into Mother's arms.

Father appeared at the door and saw us huddling together. He seemed relieved to see us all there and accounted for. "Stay here. A-a-all of you." Mother wanted to protest, but one look from him kept her silent.

I stared at the closed door after he'd vanished downstairs. A lot of commotion flooded up to us. I squirmed in my chair, and Mother vehemently shook her head. I got up nevertheless. Her trembling hand tried to grab my arm, but I was faster.

I bolted downstairs. My bike lay mangled in the hallway. I stepped over it with barely a glance and opened the front door. A brick flew past my head, and I tried to duck out of its way, but it caught me on the shoulder. I winced, and out of the corner of my eye, spotted flames lapping out of our shop.

I threw the front door shut and stumbled back into the hallway and over my bike. My breathing was weighed and labored, loud in the dark, cold hallway that had already seemed so unwelcoming and scary as a child. But for the first time in my life, it felt like the safest place.

Outside, men were yelling. A woman screamed farther off. The crashing of glass and steps on shattered fragments filled the air.

Where was Father? My gut churned knowing he was out there.

I inched closer to the door and peeked through the old rusty keyhole. People were running by. An array of debris cluttered the street and sidewalk. A thin white ribbon danced in midair, from the heat of the flames I assumed. It danced higher and higher, my restricted vision losing track of it within seconds. Then my eye fell on legs clad in military boots to the side.

Next to them lay a body.

I strained my eye, pressing it hard against the keyhole and my cheek hard against the door. I recognized the trousers and shoes.

I muffled my scream, pressing both of my hands hard on my mouth, and staggered backward, half-crawling back over my fallen bike. My arm slipped, and I hit my head.

I looked up to where my family had lived all my life, where I'd grown up, and where my mother was now waiting in fear with my little sister. I stared at the door. I wanted to run out there. I wanted to get to Father. But I knew what that could mean, so instead,

I scooted to the left, away from the bike, and leaned against the wall. I pulled my legs in and pressed my hands hard against my ears in a vain attempt to block out the terrible noises that seeped in from the outside.

My father had been beaten to death that night. When he'd come rushing out of the house, our neighbor Herr Schmidt was already trying to put out the fire set to our shop. Most likely to save his own home next door. As soon as Father had appeared in front of the store, horrified at what was happening to his livelihood, members of the SA and SS cornered him and pushed him around.

It was my father's stutter that had caused the first blow to his jaw. He hadn't answered them fast enough when they questioned if he was the owner of the shop. They had grabbed him and dragged him away, as our neighbor had reported to us the next day. While Herr Schmid had tried to save our store from the flames, the Nazi thugs were beating Father to a pulp.

My gentle father. He was gone. Forever gone. What were we going to do without him?

The store had been destroyed by bricks and fire. The whole house was lost, including the neighbor's. No one had helped him put out the flames. We'd lost everything we owned, including my Minerva.

My mother had found me in the dark hallway and ushered Clara and me out the backdoor. Her resolve had been an odd comfort to me. Under the cover of the night, we had made our way to Aunt

Irene's house, avoiding the main roads, and walking in the fields between Salzhausen and Altstädt.

When we got to Aunt Irene's, we found her house and school vandalized and ransacked. To my mother's great relief, she and Helene were unharmed. We learned the next day that Alice and her little family had miraculously been spared that night, but the synagogues in both towns had been burnt as well. Shops and businesses run by Jews had also been vandalized, and quite a few Jewish men had been arrested. Fathers, husbands, brothers, sons, and uncles.

My father was the only one that had died at the hands of the Nazis in Salzhausen and Altstädt that night.

CHAPTER 4

1939

I breathed into my frozen hands and rubbed them together, hoping the friction would help warm them up. Mother, Helene, Clara, and I huddled close together in line in front of Salzhausen's town hall with the rest of our small Jewish community, trying to keep warm on a cold January day.

While we lived with Aunt Irene since my father's death, we were still registered in Salzhausen, and all Jews of the town had been ordered to come to the town hall. The government had declared our ID cards and passports invalid, and they would only become valid again if we turned them in to be stamped with a J. They would also make a change to our names. Well, those with Germanic first names. Clara and Helene would get an added Jewish name as their middle name to make sure they could not be mistaken for Germans. Mother and I had a Jewish first name and would be spared the unwelcome addition to our names.

The irony was that the regime Would add the name Sara for all Jewish women with German names and the name Israel for all

Jewish men with a German name. In the end, my mother and my sisters and I would all bear the same name.

Helene had been outraged when Mother told us. In contrast, I'd broken out in hysterical laughter, which had made Helene even more angry. I was scolded by both Mother and Aunt Irene for my inappropriate outburst. Helene had refused to go with us to the town hall, and only Aunt Irene, who faced the same fate as her, had been able to convince her to go.

Anyone not obeying the government's directive would be arrested by the Gestapo. We had no choice.

When we returned to Altstädt, Aunt Irene greeted us at the door and quickly ushered us in. She was eager to talk to us.

"Clara can go to England," she announced while we were still taking off our winter coats. We looked at her in confusion. With a side glance at Clara who stared at her, Aunt Irene continued. "My friend Barbara, who I went to university with, sent me a letter. She works for the Reich Representation of Jews in Berlin," she said while ushering us all into the living room. "Barbara said England is accepting child refugees. They've started sending Jewish children on trains to Holland and ferrying them across. They live with English families and will return when this is all over.

"Don't you understand? We can send Clara. So she is safe." No one spoke, so she added, "And Ruth."

"Out of the question," I said with a finality that surprised even me. Aunt Irene couldn't be serious. Ruth was too young to be sent anywhere alone. Besides, Alice would never allow it. And I wouldn't either.

"Don't you see? It's getting worse by the day. We can't just sit here and await our fate," Helene chimed in. "At least Clara and Ruth have a way of getting out now. We need to send them."

Mother, who hadn't been the same since Father's death, walked over to the old sewing machine Aunt Irene had received on her fourteenth birthday but had rarely used.

She had never liked sewing but still was the proud daughter of a tailor. It had been decreed that Jews had to hand over all their valuables, among them sewing machines. Aunt Irene had defied that order, and her house had not been searched yet, perhaps because she was a teacher. When not in use, she hid it in her attic but took it out whenever we wanted or needed to sew. All our machines had perished in the fire, so we shared Aunt Irene's machine between all of us.

Mother sat down with a sigh. She pulled the thread through and started sewing. I had no idea what she was working on, but the whirring of the machine brought me comfort.

"It's not going to get better in Germany, Sara," Helene hissed in my ear.

"She's right," Aunt Irene said. She had one arm around Clara's shoulder. Turning to her, she said, "What do you think, Clara? Would you be brave enough to go? So, you're safe?"

Clara's eyes filled with tears. "I don't want to go. I want to stay with you. I'd be all alone."

"Things might get worse here, and we don't want to have to worry about you being safe. You'd come back as soon as things are better here."

"See it as a summer camp, an adventure, a trip," Helene added.

"Why can't I just go visit Bobe then?"

"Because England is safer." Aunt Irene pulled Clara over to the sofa and sat down with her, one arm still around her shoulder.

"And because they hate us in Poland, too," Helene said. I could tell she was getting impatient.

"Can't I go to Georg in America?"

"We can't afford that passage, Clara," Helene said bluntly. "And it's too far of a journey at your age. They won't let you get on a ship without an adult, silly."

"Will you go to England, Clara? Please?" Aunt Irene's gentle yet urging voice filled the room.

The sewing machine was no longer whirring. Clara looked at our mother, who looked down at her hands in her lap. Both were crying. Clara then turned to Aunt Irene. She wiped away the tears on her cheeks with the back of her hands and gave her a determined nod.

Aunt Irene squeezed her tight.

"But we can't send Ruth," I insisted.

Helene, who still stood close to me, pushed out her lower jaw. Her lip was trembling. "How can you say something so stupid."

"That's enough, Helene." Mother got up and walked toward us. A loud knock on the door froze her step.

We all looked at Aunt Irene, who got up slowly. Helene reached out to stop her. "What if—"

"It's probably just one of my students or their parents checking on me," Aunt Irene said. Her voice implied she doubted her own words, but she proceeded to the entryway nevertheless. I couldn't help but think that the knock was far too loud to be one of her students.

How times had changed. Only a few years ago, we would have been excited over a visit. Friends calling over. We would have fought over getting to the door first. Instead, we stood in silence and anxiously watched Aunt Irene approach her front door with bated breath.

I stopped breathing when she opened it. We all breathed out in collective relief when it was Alice and Hershel with little Ruth.

Aunt Irene ushered them in quickly and took their coats. Little Ruth came running over to me, and I swept her up in my arms, burying my face in her soft dark curls and holding her more tightly than usual.

In the sitting room, Hershel angrily threw his and Alice's ID cards on the table. No words were necessary.

Aunt Irene was the first to speak. As she explained again about the *Kindertransport* to England, Alice came over and took Ruth out of my arms. She was stone-faced. Only when Aunt Irene said that Clara was going, did she flinch.

"That's out of the question," Hershel said when Aunt Irene finished. It was the first time I wholeheartedly agreed with him. I looked at Alice, who was weeping silently. Was she considering sending Ruth? How could she?

I needed to speak up.

But Helene, perhaps having noticed I was about to jump in, quickly interjected instead. "You must send her, Alice! You have to!" She doubled down. "We need to save the children. We can't be selfish now."

Alice fought back more tears. "Stop, Helene. You're being cruel!" I shot her a withering look. She pushed her jaw out in defiance but held her tongue. She was not as close to Alice as me but loved her just as much.

"I agree with Hershel," I said. He looked surprised. Hershel was now almost completely bald, and I still didn't like him very much, but he was part of the family, and he loved Ruth as much as Alice. And that was enough for me. "Ruth is too young. We can't send her away to a foreign country. That's crazy." Hershel nodded in agreement, but Alice seemed torn.

"Clara would be with Ruth. She's old enough to help take care of her," Aunt Irene said. She went over to Alice and looked at her imploringly.

"What if they separate them? How can we be sure they'll stay together?" Alice's voice quivered.

"We make sure to tell them. They wouldn't separate family. I heard they keep siblings together." Aunt Irene tried to sound reassuring, but she surely also knew it was no guarantee.

"We won't send her." Hershel stepped over to Alice and Ruth and put his arm around his wife. Alice sighed in relief as if she were glad that Hershel had decided for her.

Aunt Irene looked defeated. "I understand," she said simply and sat back down on the couch next to Clara, who was staring at her hands.

She would be going alone.

"I don't understand!" Helene was almost shouting. "I don't understand how you don't want to save her."

"You wouldn't understand because you're not a mother," I snapped.

"Neither are you, Sara."

"That's enough!" It was the second time Mother had spoken up to end any impending fights. "I will make soup now," she said before rising from the machine and heading to the kitchen. Clara followed her.

I walked over to Alice, who was still holding Ruth.

"I'm scared, Sara," she whispered as she sat down. I sat next to her, unable to hide my own fears.

Ruth climbed into my lap and nestled her head against my shoulder. "Me too, Alice." But at least we would all be together. Except for Clara, who would be shipped off to another country.

Who knew when we would see her again.

———

The day the war broke out, Mother stopped making her soup. She'd lost all interest in making it, so I started to cook rosol in her stead, just as she and Bobe had shown me.

That fall, my mother's days were solely occupied with sewing and writing replies to letters that arrived every few days—from

Bobe and Zayde who wrote about the changes that had come to Chelm since the start of the German occupation. Their words were vague and never went into much detail. And then were the letters from Clara who had left us months ago in February but faithfully and obediently wrote home as we'd made her promise. While she expressed her homesickness, she sounded happy.

Of all the letters we received in those days, hers were the most comforting.

Georg also wrote more frequently, repeatedly urging us to join him in America. He'd even sent us boarding passes for a ship in early summer when rumors of Hitler's war preparations had reached America. One for each of us. It must have cost him a fortune. We'd stood in line for visas all day only to be turned away at the end of the day. We returned the next. Stood in line again. Without much success.

With the outbreak of the war in September, fewer and fewer ships were now leaving Europe, and countries issued fewer visas and accepted fewer refugees. It seemed impossible to get out now. We felt trapped. At least most of us.

Mother still refused to discuss leaving, while Helene fervently started to promote Palestine again. About fleeing there. Across borders. On foot. But the concept was more impossible than getting to America. We never considered it in earnest. It became hopeless.

We became hopeless.

CHAPTER 5

1940

Helene often came home late at night. None of us knew where she'd been. She usually just apologized for missing dinner but assured Mother that she'd eaten at a friend's or Alice's house. Our mother would then chide her for eating Alice's food, knowing they struggled like everyone else. But Helene had gotten a lot thinner; she wasn't eating enough.

She clearly had been lying. I confirmed my theory once by asking Alice if Helene was spending more evenings with them, but our eldest sister had been surprised by my question. Alice had confirmed that Helene had done so a few times but not all as often as she claimed, and Helene often left to go to a friend's house.

Helene was up to something.

One night, I stayed awake to wait for Helene to come home. I had to find out what Helene was up to.

I must have dozed off after all because I was startled awake by the door closing. I estimated it was close to midnight. Helene had just slipped into the room. She changed out of her clothes and into her nightgown. The rustling of papers followed the scratch of fabric.

"What are you doing?" I hissed at her. She froze, if the end of the rustling was any indication.

"Why are you awake?" She hissed back.

"Because you're making a ruckus!"

"Quiet," she said.

"Where have you been?" I snapped, unable to contain myself any longer. "What are you doing up so late? All the time? Where do you always go?"

Helene approached my bedside. She pressed her hand over my mouth and shushed me. I tried to pry her hand off to protest, but she proceeded to pull me out of my bed and out of the room with her. I let her; hopeful she'd tell me what she'd been up to.

"Why aren't you asleep?" She growled as soon as we were outside the room in the hallway. We were both barefoot and in our nightgowns, and the cold seeped through the linoleum up my feet and legs. I shivered and regretted not leaving it alone. Leaving Helene alone, who had her arms crossed and glowered at me. Her anger made her look less frail.

"W-where do you always go, Helene? I know y-you're up to something." Shivers made me sputter.

"It's none of your business. Why do you always have to be so nosy?" She huffed and rolled her eyes. "Maybe one day, I'll let you know but not tonight." Despite her frustration, her tone softened a little, as did her posture, but I wasn't about to let her get off so easily regardless.

"Why not now?"

"... Because I don't want to endanger you."

Anxiety as cold as the floor rose inside me. "So, it's dangerous what you're doing?" My shivers became uncontrollable.

"Sara, please. I'm keeping you all safe. And that's what matters." She placed her hand on my arm to reassure me. Or stop my shivering. I wasn't sure. But it helped a little either way.

I sighed. "I'm scared something will happen to you. You're already breaking curfew all the time. That's dangerous in itself."

"I know, but don't worry. I'm being careful. Just know that what I'm doing is for the right reasons. I'm trying to help. Make things better. Trust me, Sara. I'll tell you soon."

The promise and the cold that was now engulfing my whole body convinced me to give up pursuing an explanation. For now. I nodded and went back to the bedroom. Helene followed without a word.

I slipped into bed and rubbed my icy feet. Shuffling close by meant Helene was getting comfortable in her own bed. "Good night!" I whispered to her.

"Good night, Sara."

The warmth and weight of the thick down blanket aided my sleep, and I drifted off.

———

I stepped outside of Alice and Hershel's apartment building. The cold autumn wind caught me and tousled my hair. I buttoned up my coat and put up my collar. There was a slight drizzle in the air.

Aunt Irene's house, where we still lived, wasn't far off, so I didn't expect to get soaked, but I decided to hurry my step anyway.

When I took the next street corner, a few young people huddled close together in an alleyway across. Some of them had bikes. Congregating like that was dangerous and cause for suspicion, so I hurried along, but I caught a glimpse of a familiar sight.

Aunt Irene's bike.

I stopped and stared at the group. No one seemed to notice me standing there. It wasn't my aunt among the group, though. It was my sister.

Helene was talking passionately. Occasionally someone interrupted her, and she nodded vehemently in response. I debated if I should interrupt. Some of Helene's Jewish friends were there, too. A couple of them had been members of the Zionist youth movement while in school and were a few years older than us both.

Was Helene thinking about going to Palestine again? Would she leave us? How could she?

I started walking again, unaware that the drizzle had turned to rain. All I could think about was Helene still wanting to leave. Naively, I'd believed she'd given up on that, and things had gotten so bad recently, that it was even more dangerous to get out of Germany.

The all-too-familiar mixture of loss and fear gripped me harder than the cold autumn wind.

Helene and I were on our way to Alice's house. We'd found two trunks with clothing from the twenties in Aunt Irene's attic last week. She'd bought the house fifteen years ago and had never fully inspected or used the attic. Out of boredom and some curiosity,

Helene and I had gone up one day while Aunt Irene wasn't at home to see what treasures were stored up there.

We didn't find any treasures, just pigeon and mice droppings, but also some broken old furniture pieces and two big wooden trunks. From fancy flapper dresses and hats to ragged old coats and suits had been inside. None of it had been in style for a couple of decades.

We told Alice about our find, and she asked Aunt Irene if we could have the contents for sewing lessons. She agreed, with the stipulation that we'd make some usable articles of clothing for her students. Of course, we accepted that condition. We were grateful to have something worthwhile to do.

And I was grateful for the opportunity to spend some time with Helene to again try to find out what she was up to.

"I saw you the other day. In the alley. With your friends," I said when we entered Alice's street.

Helene stopped in her tracks and looked at me, her face unreadable.

"I know what you're up to." I searched her face, which yielded no clues, to my frustration.

"What do you think I'm up to, Sara?" she asked coldly.

I scanned our surroundings. We were alone, but I proceeded to whisper it in her ear anyway. When I looked at her face again, she was smiling. I narrowed my eyes.

"Oh, Sara," she said with a hint of annoyance and pulled me closer. As I'd done, she whispered in my ear. "We aren't trying to leave. We've formed a resistance."

"What?! Why would you do something so dangerous?" I yelled.

"Shhhh."

I looked over my shoulder and scanned the sidewalk behind us. Snow had accumulated, but only our footprints were visible. We were completely alone. I lifted my eyes to the gray sky above, and snowflakes caressed my face.

It was early in the morning and the air was cold and heavy with moisture. Winter had come early. It was only early November, and we'd seen snow twice already.

"Why would you become part of such a group? It's not only putting yourself but all of us in great danger! You said you were trying to protect us!" Did Aunt Irene know? Alice? Certainly not Mother.

"I'm being careful," she said, trying to calm me. "We have a radio. It's hidden. I won't tell you where. But we listen to the BBC whenever we can. My friend studied English at the university. He translates what we learn about the war, and we write it up and make copies. I learned some English in the process."

I couldn't shake the uneasiness curling in my gut. Helene was so nonchalant about it. As if it wasn't dangerous at all. "What if you get caught?" I said, unwilling to hide my anxiety. We were almost at Alice's apartment, but I needed more details. "What do you do with the copies, and where do you get the paper?" I asked while pulling Helene to a stop.

She turned to me while checking our surroundings. "We leave them on benches at the park and drop them in mailboxes. Believe it or not, Hershel is helping us."

My jaw dropped. "D-does Alice know?" I stammered. I couldn't picture Hershel Wolf as a resistance fighter or even tolerating such activities. Nor could I imagine Alice ever lying about knowing.

Helene didn't answer my question but pulled me inside the building and up the stairs to Alice's and Hershel's apartment. Before knocking on their door, Helene shot me a warning look. "Not a word!"

I nodded reluctantly, frowning.

———

It was Hanukkah, and Alice, Helene, Aunt Irene, and I were loading a hand-drawn wooden wagon we'd borrowed from my aunt's neighbor to deliver clothes to the homes of Helene's and Aunt Irene's students. We'd altered the clothes found in my aunt's attic for weeks with the goal of delivering them just in time for the holiday to bring some cheer to the few Jewish families of Altstädt. Even my aunt, who rarely sewed, had helped.

The four of us made our way to Main Street where we'd start our distribution. Nothing would be more rewarding than the joy and gratitude on people's faces when they receive the clothing we'd toiled over. We stopped with our wagon in front of the first house.

A Star of David branded the front door, but it was no longer an unusual sight.

We knocked, but no one answered. We knocked again. Helene proceeded to peek inside the windows. She reported that the living room looked deserted.

"Maybe they left?" Aunt Irene suggested. "They did talk about leaving."

"They had the right idea," Helene gave back.

"It's not that we haven't tried, Helene," I said.

"People go into hiding, too. Maybe that's what they—"

"What?" We stared at Alice. She was usually the last to know anything. "Hide where?" I asked.

"In basements, the forest, barns," Alice said. "People are afraid to get arrested. So, they hide."

In forests? I shook my head at that idea as we pulled our wagon away from the house and down the street. No one could survive in the forest for long. What would they eat? Mushrooms, berries? And where would people sleep? It was December. No one would survive living out in the cold. Nor could I imagine anyone choosing to do so.

Too many rumors had been flying around. And one seemed more ludicrous than the other. People were scared and fear made them say and believe anything.

We arrived at the next house minutes later and were able to deliver some of the clothing. The family of four was grateful for our gift and invited us in for some tea. We gladly accepted to get out of the cold for a few minutes. The two daughters, two lovely girls only a year apart, had been Aunt Irene's students. We could tell how grateful they were for the diversion our little visit brought. They happily chatted with us while their parents sat in silent somberness.

Aunt Irene noticed their quietness and turned to them. "Have you gotten any news from your family in Poland?" She asked. The father looked at her wide-eyed, then at his two girls.

"Why don't we try these clothes on? See how they fit?" I said to the girls. "We can alter them if they don't." I draped the articles of clothing over my arm and ushered the two girls out of the room so the parents could speak freely.

We left the family's home twenty minutes later. As soon as we were back on the sidewalk pulling our wagon, I asked for a report. I'd been the only one not privy to the conversation.

"Things in Poland aren't good," Aunt Irene said with a lowered gaze. "Especially for our people," she added. I looked at my sisters. They didn't look at me either, their eyes also fastened on the ground.

"There is no more Poland, remember?" Helene said. We'd all heard Poland had been divided up between Germany and the Soviet Union. My grandparents in Chelm were now part of the Reich.

"But what does that mean exactly? That things are not good for our people?" I asked.

"They're segregating the Jews. Forcing them out of their homes into ghettos," Aunt Irene said.

"And murdering them," Helene added.

I frowned at Helene. She always had to be so crass and matter-of-fact.

All I could think about was Bobe and Zayde. I hoped they were safe. Mother grew more worried for them with each passing day, and so did I. I was worried for them and all of us.

CHAPTER 6

1941

"Another letter from Bobe," Helene said, waving an envelope around as she strode through the door. She was returning from one of her attempts to secure potatoes from the local farmer who'd attended school with Father and who had remained friends with him until his death. I think the farmer felt bad for our family, and sharing some of his potatoes with us was his way of honoring his old friend, even if that friend had been a Jew.

It was early March, still winter, and the few potatoes Helene let roll onto the kitchen table had numerous sprouts and visible marks of deterioration. But we were grateful for the farmer sharing whatever he had left in his cellar regardless.

Mother ignored the potatoes and took the letter from Helene. With a swift and impatient movement, she opened it. Then she sank onto a chair, and we gathered around her. We silently read Bobe's letter together.

My grandmother wrote that she and Zayde had been forced out of their home. She said a part of Chelm had been turned into restricted quarters, a ghetto, confirming what we'd learned from the Jewish family to whom we'd delivered clothes. Bobe didn't give too much detail about the ghetto where they had been relocated to or daily life there. But she had underlined some words, which made things clear without specific details. They weren't allowed to leave and return to their home.

I couldn't picture Zayde not on his little bench in front of their house.

Mother wept. It had been the home where she'd been born and grew up. Where my sisters and I had spent many summers.

Bobe's letter left us distraught and even more worried. Her lines had tried to reassure us that they were well and had enough food to eat, but none of us believed it. We knew better, and we knew Bobe.

I stared at the end of the letter where Bobe had written their new address in her best handwriting to make sure we would get it correct when we wrote to her. Around the address, she'd drawn a box with a star of David on each corner.

I thought of the golem and wondered if anyone could sneak into the attic of the synagogue and resurrect him to protect the Jews of Chelm. While the story of the golem had caused me nightmares after Bobe had told it to me that one summer, the golem no longer seemed so scary.

"I'm not going to wear that." Helene threw the piece of fabric down on the floor and crossed her arms. Mother carefully picked it up and put it back on a small pile to her right. She'd been sitting at the sewing machine all morning, making Stars of David for each of us from scrap fabric. As mandated by the government, we were now supposed to wear that yellow star visibly whenever we left the house. Little Ruth would be old enough and forced to do so in only a few months as well. At least Clara in England was spared that new humiliation.

I hated it as much as Helene. To be marked in public. Everyone in town knew we were Jews. No one needed another reminder. I put my book aside and walked over to Mother. I placed my hand on her shoulder. She in turn patted my fingers.

I looked at the yellow stars she had already sewn. How much effort she'd put into them. Why? "They look perfect!" I said, rubbing my thumb across the perfect stitches along the edges of one of the new emblems. "Too perfect for what they are for," I added.

"It's Star of David, Sara. Is meant to be perfect. It must be perfect. How can I not make it perfect?" My mother didn't look up.

"How will we fasten them onto our clothing? Are we just going to sew them on like a patch?"

"We could just use safety pin," she suggested.

I'd prefer that. I'd rather not have a badge like that sewn onto my coat permanently.

On the anniversary of Father's death, we went to the Jewish cemetery in Salzhausen to place rocks on his gravestone and honor his memory. It was a cold, drizzly, and windy November day. It was the kind of day people preferred to spend indoors. The fields lay cold and barren. Here and there, a crow cawed. We wore our coats with the collars up and the bright yellow star branded on them. Even Helene didn't complain anymore and had resigned to wearing it like the rest of us.

We had only been stopped and asked for our papers once on the way.

The tall trees that would have shaded the graves on a sunny day swayed and groaned, leafless in the wind. A murder of crows occupied the tree under which Father's grave was situated.

We huddled together in front of it, staring at the Hebrew lettering. I thought of Father. Tried to picture him. In his workshop. But I couldn't. The only image that kept flooding my mind was his beaten body. The image only left me when Mother spoke a Yiddish blessing. Aunt Irene said one, too.

Afterward, we searched for pebbles and, one by one, we placed them on Father's gravestone. Mother went last. For a moment, she rested her hand on the cold stone and wept. She opened her purse and pulled out a kerchief to dry her tears. When she closed the purse with a loud click, the crows cawed and flew off.

Their ruckus and the cold drizzle cut our visit on Father's *Yahrzeit* short.

CHAPTER 7

1942

"And?" Mother cornered me as soon as I'd come in from an afternoon at Alice's. "Any mail? Speak, child!"

I lowered my eyes and shook my head. We hadn't heard from Bobe or Zayde in months. Their letters usually arrived weekly or bi-weekly at the least. But they'd stopped coming. And Mother grew more restless and anxious by the day.

She went over to the table, sat down, and began to write yet another letter. Would that one reach its addressees? I watched her as she silently wept while writing to her parents. She paused suddenly and looked at me. "I must write my cousin. He must know something. Quick, Sara, bring my notebook. His address is somewhere in there."

I went over to the cabinet and pulled out the left drawer.

"Not that one. Other one."

Before I closed the drawer fully, my eyes fell onto what looked like ship passes. I glanced over my shoulder at my mother who was focused on the stationary in front of her and pulled the drawer back out to reach in. I stared at the papers in my hand.

"Sara!" Mother was at my side. She took them out of my hand and shoved them back inside the drawer. "You were not supposed to see," she said.

"What are those for? And for whom?" I stared at her. "I don't underst—"

"They were for you and Helene. To go to Palestine."

"How did you get the money for—"

"After your father's death ... Irene and me ... we put money together to send you to Palestine."

I could only stare at her. Did Helene know? Of course not. She'd be furious to know she'd been so close to going. She'd always advocated immigrating there. But she was a Zionist youth, and I didn't think anyone was taking her seriously. Maybe Aunt Irene, but definitely not Mother. I was speechless.

"They are useless now," Mother said. "Don't you tell Helene." She raised her finger.

"I won't. Promise."

She opened the right drawer and pulled out an old notebook. My mother flipped through the pages and found what she'd been looking for. She returned to her stationary and started another letter. To her cousin, I assumed.

I wished I could talk to someone about my find. I could ask Aunt Irene about it, but what was the use? Helene and I wouldn't be going.

For a moment, I felt what Clara must have felt when we'd all agreed to send her away. Mother had wanted to send us away. To

Palestine. Far away. While Helene would have been ecstatic, I would have refused to go.

Of that, I was sure.

———

I remember the day the letter from my mother's cousin arrived. It was an unusually hot day for late summer. We couldn't find any relief from the oppressive heat and were sitting in the shade behind Aunt Irene's house, trying to cool off with wet rags on the back of our necks and our feet in buckets of cold water.

Mother's letter had not reached her cousin directly or in any timely fashion. It had been passed from hand to hand and traversed hundreds of miles before it had eventually reached him. It had been a small miracle that it had made it to him. Someone had brought it, together with news about his family, from Chelm to the Soviet Union where he'd fled to and had joined the Red Army. Once he had received Mother's letter and had learned about his own family's fate, he'd not immediately sent a reply, which he profusely apologized for in his letter once he finally put pen to paper.

It was Alice who had brought his letter that day. She came running with it, knowing how eagerly and long our mother had waited for it. Mother tried to get her feet out of the bucket and up from her chair, but Alice had hastily placed it in her lap before she could. We tried to hover around her as we usually did to read the letter together, but she held up her arms. Helene and I wanted to protest, but Aunt Irene quieted us with a shake of her head. We complied. We understood how important that letter was to Mother, but why didn't she want us to read it too?

We watched Mother intently. Her eyes flew across the stationary. She started breathing rapidly. Her face contorted into a grimace. I grabbed Helene's arm. Mother's hand flew to her mouth, trying to muffle a scream without success. I'd never heard a human scream like that, like a wounded animal. She got up and knocked over the bucket.

I stared at the spilled water darkening the ground and seeping into the earth. Helene hugged me tightly from the side. I didn't move. I didn't hug her back. I stared at the wet ground, trying to make sense of what I had just witnessed.

Somehow, the letter ended up in Aunt Irene's hand. She began to read it out loud. Her Yiddish wasn't the best, and she read haltingly. We didn't understand everything, but we understood enough.

Bobe and Zayde were gone.

Mother's cousin had found out that my grandparents had been deported from the Chelm ghetto in May to a place called Sobibor, a camp. We'd never heard of it, but it was a place, as Mother's cousin wrote, where Jews were murdered.

Aunt Irene sank onto a chair and buried her face in her hands. Helene and I grabbed each other's arms. All of us were crying. We both loved Bobe and Zayde so much. The thought of them being murdered made my stomach twist.

I let go of Helene and bent over, vomiting.

———

The loud bang on the door startled us all out of our restless sleep.

"Open the door," a voice barked, and a fist banged loudly again against the windowpane of Alice's and Hershel's apartment door. Alice and Ruth trembled next to me. I put my arm around them, shaking uncontrollably too.

In the dark, I could make out Hershel getting up from the chair he'd slept in. He'd asked me to spend the night. I hadn't questioned why. Alice had asked me sometimes if I wanted to stay over, and oftentimes, I had. When Hershel, however, had insisted on me sleeping in their bed with Alice and Ruth while he would take the big old armchair in the corner of their bedroom, I had grown suspicious.

I'd pulled him aside while Alice was in the bathroom with Ruth, but he'd been evasive. He'd seemed to be trying to hide his nervousness. He was worried about something.

Hershel came over to us, planted a kiss on both Alice's and Ruth's foreheads and left the room. I heard him turn the key and open the door. There was a scuffle. I held my breath. So too did Alice, beside me. Ruth lay perfectly still. Then the bedroom door flew open, and the light was thrown on. I gasped. Alice and I covered our eyes against the stark brightness. Ruth remained still, completely hidden under the blanket.

"Get up!" they barked.

One of the soldiers grabbed my arm and pulled me off the bed. Ruth held on to me tightly and was consequently pulled off with me. I'd hoped she would have stayed hidden, but escaping a search of the whole house would have probably been impossible. They were tearing at the mattress and overturning it while we watched, standing at the foot of the bed in our nightgowns.

The three Gestapo men who'd entered the bedroom were wearing long leather coats and military boots. Their faces matched their menacing get-up. What would they do to us?

Alice and Ruth were shaking next to me. Liquid trickled onto the floor; Ruth was wetting herself. She started to cry. Before I had the chance to comfort her, one of the men slapped her so hard, she flew against the bed. Alice screamed.

I didn't think. The sudden onset of rage not only surprised me but also the officer that I'd pushed back violently.

The fist that hit my stomach took my breath away and made me crumple to the floor. They dragged me up, out of the room, and down the stairs. My feet didn't find any hold.

They threw me in the back of a military truck where Hershel and others were already sitting or standing. Some of the people in the vehicle had bloody noses and cracked lips and brows. I cowered next to Hershel, who looked at me with anxious expectation.

"They are fine," I lied. How could I tell Hershel that they'd hurt Ruth?

The truck jerked forward, and we drove off into the unknowing dark of night. The only light that shone onto the wet cobble-stoned street behind us from apartment windows.

I clasped a hand around the necklace hanging from my neck.

I looked at Hershel. That had been why he'd asked me to stay the night. He'd expected the Gestapo. Their group had been found out. *Helene!* I mouthed.

He lowered his eyes to the floor of the truck, and my stomach dropped.

They'd be coming for her, too.

———————

I shivered under the thin blanket and turned my face toward the tiled glass window. It was almost morning. I hadn't slept much and only occasionally dozed off, despite my exhaustion from the night's events and the interrogation I'd been subjected to upon arriving at the prison.

They had screamed at and threatened me. I'd been helpless and at their mercy. Once they'd finally put me in the cell, the fear for my loved ones and not knowing what would happen next had kept me awake.

I pulled my knees in closer and hugged them for warmth and comfort. I tried to swallow the tears that threatened to well up again.

A key rattled the door open. It wasn't even day yet, and they came for me. What would they do? I wasn't sure I could bear another interrogation; the screaming, the threats. The Gestapo had to know I wasn't involved with Hershel's and Helene's group.

I looked up. Another prisoner was pushed into my cell. I'd been confined alone until that moment. The woman stumbled over to my bed and sat down. Who—

"It's me!" Helene searched my face.

I stared as if she weren't real. An apparition. A ghost. I must have dozed off after all. But she put her hand on my shoulder and her touch was too real. I threw the blanket back, jumped up, and hugged her tight.

She winced. "Ouch! I think they broke a couple of my rips."

———————

Helene told me everything, how their group had been found out, and how she'd ended up in my prison cell. Two members of their little resistance group had traveled by train with a stack of leaflets in one of their bags. I was horrified at their carelessness. Helene said that usually those who helped distribute the flyers would hide them under their clothing, but one of the two misjudged. The conductor of the train had asked for their tickets while two members of the Gestapo accompanying him had demanded their identification papers.

When the Gestapo had asked to search their bags, the one with the flyers in her bag panicked. In her distress, she'd quickly pulled them out of her bag and tried to throw them out the window, but she hadn't been fast enough. The Gestapo had caught some of the leaflets and arrested the two of them to torture the names of other members of the group out of them.

I wondered if it had been the same prison Helene and I found ourselves in.

My sister hadn't heard anything of my or Hershel's arrests. No one had told her. And no one had warned her that they would come for her.

I interrupted and told her that I believed Hershel had known because he seemingly had expected the Gestapo to show up at his apartment. Helene's brow furrowed, but she continued her story.

She explained that she had been on her way home to Aunt Irene's house when a truck had pulled up next to her. Two men had asked for her papers and arrested her on the spot.

I thanked the heavens that she hadn't reached the house. So, Mother and Aunt Irene were likely safe then.

Or at least, I hoped so.

───

The next morning, they pulled us out of our cells without any warning or word and loaded us and a group of about twenty other women prisoners onto a truck. We had no idea where we were going. One of the prisoners speculated that we were being shipped off to a labor camp in the East.

I thought of Bobe and Zayde. They had been deported to the East.

Helene seemed to think the same because she grabbed my hand and held it painfully tight as we rumbled down the street.

We arrived at a train station in pouring rain. Female guards were waiting for us at the platform, screaming at us to get onto train cars meant for animals or cargo, not humans. Remnants of straw littered the floor, and I caught a whiff of a stench I couldn't place. We climbed up into the dark cattle cars and found others already there.

All passengers were women. Young girls, barely twelve, to women in their forties, I estimated.

I held onto Helene's arm. We had to make sure not to lose each other. No matter what. We had to stay together.

A guard came by and surveyed the inside of our car. With a disgusted look at us, she crashed the door shut. Darkness enveloped us. Little light fell in through the wooden slats of the cattle car.

The train jerked forward, and I bumped into a woman next to me. She was crying. My throat tightened and my anxiety rose.

———————

The train ride took only a few hours. So, we were probably still in the Reich. They hadn't shipped us off to the East. I was a little relieved.

When the door slid open, female guards were yelling at us to get off. Helene took my hand, and we scrambled out, shielding our eyes from the light.

A loud, barking voice on a megaphone greeted us. "You're at the Ravensbrück women's prisoner camp. Those of you with nursing, sewing, or farming skills, come over here to me. If you're a gypsy or have health issues, line up over there by the wall."

Helene and I looked at each other. I quickly pulled her with me to where the guard with the megaphone was standing on a little box, clipboard in hand.

Others joined us.

She took down our names and skills. Those of us with sewing skills were lined up and marched off. I'd never marched before and had trouble falling in step. It came naturally to Helene. I wondered if she'd practiced with her resistance group. She quietly started counting, and the rhythm of it helped me fall in step with the rest of the column as we passed fences and barracks.

Women in striped uniforms working in nearby plots only briefly looked up at us. Their cheeks were hollow, their eyes empty. I involuntarily shuddered.

We stopped in front of a building where we were issued our own coarse uniforms and handed a number stenciled on a strip of fabric and triangle emblems we were told to fasten to our uniforms. The smell of the fabric repulsed me. They hadn't been washed.

I looked at Helene, who was already changing into trousers, her face grim. I followed suit, swallowing my disgust and panic. I was only glad about one thing.

That Helene was with me.

After we finished dressing, the female guards marched us to a barrack where our *Kapo* greeted us. I studied the emblems on her uniform. They were the same as ours.

"She's a political prisoner like us," Helene whispered. How had she deciphered the meaning of the patches so quickly?

The *Kapo* pointed to the barracks behind her and shouted in her shrill voice that that was where we would be housed. She explained that there was one wash basin and a few latrines for our block. I stared at the long building, trying to estimate how many people would fit in there and needed to share the facilities.

There were about 100 of us here.

When we entered our block, we found it already at capacity.

I looked at Helene, horrified. My sister's face was unreadable.

Inside, 3-tier wooden bunk beds lined each side. The smell was horrid. I covered my face with the sleeve of the dirty uniform, disturbingly preferring the scent of the fabric over that of the block. From the bunks, hollow faces stared at us. None of them seemed welcoming nor pleased to see new arrivals.

The *Kapo* assigned Helene and me to a bunk that was already shared by a mother and her fourteen-year-old daughter. They moved to one side of the bunk and nodded a shy welcome when we climbed in.

I woke up dazed the next morning to a salve of shouts. For the first few minutes, I was disoriented and questioned where I was. How I'd been able to sleep and end up somewhat rested was a mystery. Perhaps the shock of everything had knocked me out. I piled out of our beds.

The *Kapo* went through the aisle and asked if there were any dead to be collected. Helene and I stared at each other. One after another, hands shot up, indicating that someone had indeed died in their bunk during the night. I stifled a gasp at the number of hands that rose.

We were marched out of the barracks before any bodies were collected.

Outside, several women from our block were marched to the textile workshop. When we entered the building, I grabbed Helene's hand. The workshop was filled with rows upon rows of tables with sewing machines. Helene looked at me, her face a mixture of emotions.

We were assigned a seat. Luckily, Helene was seated at the station right behind me. I sighed in relief.

Some of the women were already sitting and looking at their machines nervously. Did they not know how to use them? It dawned on me that some here might have claimed sewing skills without possessing them, hoping for a better work assignment. The woman in front of me was shaking. I swallowed.

An SS officer appeared, accompanied by two female guards. "You are here to work. You will contribute to the Reich's textile industry." He paused and looked around. He wore an immaculate uniform. His chest was pushed out and he looked arrogantly at us. "Whatever you're sewing here, will support the Fuhrer's war efforts and the German men fighting valiantly on all fronts," he continued. "The Reich needs you, and as long as you do as told, no harm will come to you."

He turned and walked off into a room to the side that was only separated by a glass wall. Behind the glass, he sat down and took off his hat. He lit a cigarette and began reading a paper as if he weren't presiding over a room full of prisoners.

The two female guards had remained with us and were joined by four prisoners. They were introduced as our *Anweisers* who would instruct us in the sewing of military garments for the Wehrmacht. Helene shifted in her seat behind me. She probably never imagined having to sew uniforms for the very people her resistance defied. I swallowed hard to suppress a hysterical giggle at the irony.

The sewing machines had already been set up and were ready to go. Our *Anweisers* brought us heavy fabric that had been cut in patterns, and we were ordered to gather around and watch how to sew the patterns into a military uniform jacket. Helene and I only half paid attention because the task wouldn't be challenging for us. But there were a few women watching whose faces showed full unabated concentration, including the one who had been seated in front of me. She was biting her lips and watching carefully while kneading her hands.

After the demonstration, she moved closer to me and asked me quietly if I could help her if needed. I nodded encouragingly.

We went back to our stations and were told that we had to fulfill a certain quota for the day and that the quota would be increased with each day for the coming week. I hoped Helene and I would be able to keep up. We'd never had to sew under duress.

I could only imagine how the woman in front of me felt. I'd help her, but I wasn't sure how much I'd be able to do. We were watched closely. The two female guards would keep an eye on us throughout the day, going up and down the rows to ensure we were working.

Soon, a familiar whirring filled the air, but I'd never heard so many machines at the same time. It was almost exhilarating. Almost.

My first jacket turned out well, and I caught myself looking at my work with pride. I chastised myself, but I hadn't sewn in months, and it felt like home to me to run the machine and let the fabric glide through my fingers.

Helene behind me finished soon after. Our *Anweiser* came over and gave a satisfied nod and handed us more fabric. When she went past the woman in front of me, though, she stopped.

"What is this? What are you doing? You're wasting fabric. Can you even sew?" The woman looked up at her, tears streaming down her face. The *Anweiser* leaned in. "Stop!" She hissed. "You're getting the fabric all wet."

My heart raced as I watched from the corner of my eye. What would happen?

The instructor looked around for the guards who were on either end of the workshop before whispering, "This is how you do it." She bent down and helped the woman. "If you aren't able to learn quickly, very quickly, you'll be found out," she murmured and left.

With trembling fingers, the woman in front of me moved the fabric, but her needle caught.

"You can't go too slow. Go faster. Keep a steady speed," I whispered, leaning forward.

"No talking," the guard yelled from behind me. I quickly sat back and started on my second jacket.

The instructor and I tried to help the woman in front of me whenever we could, but it wasn't enough. After two days, she was gone, and another prisoner occupied her station. I no longer saw her in our barracks either. Guilt coiled in my gut about not having been able to help her more.

I asked Helene at the end of the second day while visiting the latrines if she'd seen her. She shook her head, her face hard.

"She's probably been assigned to a different work detail," I wondered out loud, hoping that it was true.

"Or shot," my sister said without looking at me.

"Helene!" I hissed.

She looked at me and rolled her eyes. "Don't be naive, Sara. If people aren't of any use to the Reich, the SS gets rid of them. They shoot people daily. How can you be so ignorant?"

It wasn't ignorance. I was just hoping for another possibility.

Why did Helene always have to be so harsh? Growing up with her, I knew how she could get when she was hungry. And we were hungry. All the time. Every minute of the day and night but that was cold and unfeeling of her to say. Was the camp already changing her? I refused to give in to the brutality around us.

"Sara, we are slaves to the Reich. And we're helping them with their war. Every day, all day. I'd rather be on a different work detail."

"Who is naive here, Helene?" I snapped. "We work inside. We sit all day. Do you even realize—see and hear what other prisoners have to do? How can you say such a thing?" We were lucky. I'd realized that when I'd passed the women digging ditches in the cold and rain on our first day. Helene needed to realize that it could be worse. Much worse. Knowing how to sew had spared us that fate.

"I know that," Helene mumbled, a hint of defensiveness in her voice.

Time passed us by. Often, I was unaware what day it was. It didn't matter. One was the same as the next. We worked from early morning to late night in the camp's textile workshop. In the evening, we returned to our barracks with aching backs and fingers and fell into an exhausted sleep.

We had learned that our bunkmates had been deported from Vienna to Ravensbrück almost a month ago. They were working in the camp's yard, digging ditches. The mother and daughter were friendly but mostly kept to themselves. Helene and I observed how the mother frequently gave her rations, which consisted of a slice of bread and imitation coffee in the morning and a bowl of watery vegetable soup for lunch and dinner, to her daughter who protested at first, but with the passing days and weeks, no longer resisted. The mother wasted away in front of our eyes, but we were so exhausted and consumed with our own hunger that we had no strength to convince her to stop giving up her rations.

She was a mother. Our mother would have done the same. We understood.

After more than a week in the camp, I'd accepted our fate. I began to grow numb. The sheer exhaustion had made me despondent. Not Helene, though. Sitting behind me, she consistently muttered under her breath. She had a hard time accepting that she was now part of the war machine. Forced laborers.

At the end of another long day, Helene's muttering was overheard by the overseeing guard passing through the rows. I held my breath when the guard stopped right next to my sister's workstation. I squeezed my eyes shut and held my breath, expecting the worst.

"Shut up," the guard barked at my sister.

There was a crack of the guard's club, and Helene whined. Out of the corner of my eye, I saw Helene being pulled up and out of her chair by her hair. The guard dragged her over to the administrative room, where the scene that unfolded was closely watched by the SS officer from behind the glass.

I wanted to get up. Run after her. Help her. But instead, I sat frozen in place, fear paralyzing me.

Silence was settling over the workshop. Most sewing machines had stopped whirring. We all stared at Helene who was now on the other side of the window glass. I didn't dare blink to not lose sight of her.

With atypical slumped over shoulders, she stood in front of the SS officer with the guard by her side. The officer got up and began to yell abuse at her. We could all hear it. I feared the worst. In frozen stillness, I sat there, completely helpless, hoping my sister wouldn't be dragged off to be shot. I couldn't lose another member of my family. I wouldn't survive it. But there was nothing I could do to prevent that from happening, and the consequences for interfering would probably be even worse.

I tore my eyes off my sister and lowered my gaze, staring at the sewing machine. "Please, please," I whispered to myself, hoping the relentless yelling would stop and Helene would return to me.

I breathed out in relief when the officer finally fell silent. I looked back up. He was seated again as he dismissed Helene with a wave of his hand.

The female guard pushed her out of the room and back to her place in front of the sewing machine. The frantic whirring of sewing machines arose again. I welcomed it.

A minute later, Helene's sewing machine joined the chorus.

That night, lying on her stomach to give her back some relief, Helene suggested we needed to find a way to sabotage the production of the military garments. I told her it was too dangerous and reminded her of what had happened today at the workshop, only because she simply had muttered to herself. But Helene was Helene. She insisted that it was our duty to resist. I reminded her that it was our duty to survive. For Mother. For our family. But she didn't hear me.

She promised that she would come up with a plan, and she made me promise that I would follow it once she did. I nodded, but it was at that moment, at the end of that day when I almost lost my sister, I'd promised myself that I would have my own plan. A plan that would ensure we both survived and would go home one day.

It was soon discovered that Helene and I were very skilled. I for one easily matched the daily assigned quota by early afternoon, and the instructor always gave a satisfied grunt upon inspecting the finished products.

After two weeks in Ravenbrück, it was my turn to stand in front of the SS officer but for different reasons. I had been summoned to his office. The guard escorted me from my station, and I went behind the glass wall. I folded my hands to keep them from trembling.

The SS officer told me that because of my great abilities, I was ordered to become an *Anweiser* which included ensuring quality production, fixing any mistakes made, ensuring the overall quota was met, and instructing and training new arrivals. I nodded in agreement and was led out of his office.

From that day on, I was no longer sitting all day in front of my sewing machine. Though sitting all day was better than the back-breaking physical labor other prisoners had to endure outside under any condition and in any weather. While I was looking forward to having varied tasks, I was also keenly aware that I was no longer working right in front of Helene, and I also fully comprehended that the heightened responsibility also meant more danger.

If I failed, it could mean severe punishment.

And how would I keep Helene safe? We needed to stay together. No matter what. But my station was occupied by another woman while I and the other instructor occupied a large table in the back of the workshop that had a pair of sewing machines on it.

A major part of that worktable was used by us to cut out patterns. A mountain of camouflage and heavy green fabric was stacked in the nearby corner. Scraps of fabric littered the floor around and under the big table, which we had to clean up at the end of the day.

The SS's concern about order, neatness, and cleanliness stood in stark contrast to my father's workshop. It had been a place of creativity where we had been surrounded by chaos of fabric, thread, fashion magazines, and tools. My father had been neat and perfect in his sewing, but his workshop had been another story. And we'd all felt at home in there. The sterile and hostile space in the textile workshop didn't allow for any creativity and homeliness.

Helene had always been the better seamstress than me and should have been promoted, but my sister also purposefully worked slower to barely meet the daily quota. She played a dangerous game. She mocked me mercilessly over my "promotion," ridiculing and chastising me relentlessly for my "contributions to the war effort." As if I had a choice.

She knew I had none. But she also, without fail, advised me daily on how to make sure everyone met the quota, where to cut corners without being discovered, and how to ensure my fellow seamstresses made it through the day. At least Helene seemed to slowly realize that sabotage was not a good option with my life on the line, so she eventually gave up scheming for my sake and supported me in looking out for everyone who worked on our floor.

After two and a half weeks in the camp, it was Helene's and my turn to carry the soup in a large metal pail from the camp kitchen to our barracks for distribution after a day's work for dinner. It was excruciating work in our weakened state. Filled to the rim, the food pail weighed close to fifty kilograms, and we had to make sure none of it spilled. It was a slow and agonizing walk, but we managed.

Every drop of the disgusting brew was precious and meant life.

Those who carried the soup also had the task of dishing it out to their fellow prisoners. It was a task I'd dreaded even more than carrying the heavy pail. I'd witnessed food envy at distribution before. It had gotten ugly more than once. I begged Helene to fill the bowls while I handed them back. She agreed with a grim face, fully aware of the precariousness of the task.

When Helene had filled the bowl of our fourteen-year-old bunkmate, I handed it back to her with the encouraging words of sharing it with her mother and coming back for another ration for her. Those standing around me waiting for their turn had overheard my instructions and started to complain. I ignored them, and they settled down. However, when the girl returned for another serving, the murmurs around me broke out again.

Helene took the girl's bowl and filled it. When I took it from my sister to pass it on to the girl, a blow hit the side of my head. I dropped to the floor. The soup splattered beneath me.

My head hammered when I came back to it. I looked at the feet standing around me, fully expecting another blow. A few pieces of vegetables lay strewn about, the remnants of an invaluable meal. Helene was yelling at people to get away and give me room to breathe. She crouched down and pulled me up with her. Something wet and warm trickled down my temple.

Then everything went black.

I found myself on the floor of our block with my head resting in my sister's lap. My shoes were gone. Helene's hand was resting on top of the wet cloth on my forehead.

"How are you feeling? How's your head?" She seemed to be trying to keep the concern out of her voice, but I knew her too well.

"I'm fine," I said as I tried to sit up. The searing headache was worse in an upright position, but I wanted to get off the floor and into the bed. Most people around us were already asleep. No one paid attention to us. "Who was it?" I whispered.

"Why does it matter?"

"It matters. Tell me who."

"It was the *Kapo*." She looked past me toward the door as if she was expecting someone. Helene knew I wouldn't be able to stand up to the *Kapo* without any serious repercussions. *Kapos* were privileged and brutal and used their position of authority to their advantage. It was never a good idea to get the *Kapo* on your bad side. But had Helene lied to me? I wasn't sure.

I studied her, but her face was unreadable.

"Let's get you to bed." She helped ease me into a standing position and into bed.

The fourteen-year-old girl looked at me with big eyes when I lay down, but I ignored her and her mother. I was nursing a splitting headache because of her, and all I wanted was to close my eyes and block out the world around me.

After a month in Ravensbrück, one night, when we arrived back in our barracks, tired from a day at the workshop, we found our teenage bunkmate distraught. Her mother's emaciated body was gasping for air. The rattle in her breaths, for each of which she was battling, told us she wouldn't make it. The mother's face was flushed with fever.

I put my hand on the girl's shoulder and shook my head. She buried her face in her hands and sobbed uncontrollably. I gently moved her over to her mother and placed the woman's hand, clammy and fragile, into the girl's. "Hold her. She needs to know you're here with her," I said. I was surprised at my own calm. I'd never seen a person die before. Father had been killed before I spotted his body, but to witness someone taking their last breaths felt surprisingly ordinary.

That night, Helene and I slept on a blanket on the hard and dirty floor of the barracks. We had to give the girl and her mother the privacy they needed. I also didn't feel like waking up next to a corpse. And Helene was concerned we might catch whatever was finishing the mother off.

Disease was spreading wildly all around us. The neighboring barracks had had a typhus outbreak. Helene and I had grown wary of any cough or fever around us. A night on the floor was the safest option.

The next morning, the girl's mother was dead. Her daughter didn't even have the strength to cry. She looked blankly at the corpse. I tried to avoid looking at the body. I was numb and would be of little comfort to the girl.

Helene told me to keep her company while she went to get the *Kapo*. After the *Kapo* and a female guard had determined that the woman was indeed dead, she ordered two prisoners to remove the body and take it to the collection station. That was a common routine. Someone would always succumb during the night in our block, but up until today, I'd managed not to face the corpses that were carried out. I usually left the barracks beforehand or took great care to avoid looking at them.

Usually, it was more than one person. The *Kapo* would assign two prisoners to carry them outside and transport them in a common wheelbarrow to the collection place. Death no longer surprised or shocked us. I'd grown cold to it. I hated myself for it, but I had no more tears left.

The night would make its cut, and the bodies of the dead were thrown into piles to be transported to the nearby Fürstenberg camp, where the corpses would be reduced to ashes in its crematorium. Rumors were flying that Ravensbrück would soon have its own crematorium. More people were dying every day, especially with the repeated outbreaks of typhus.

―――――――

"Did you hear? Today, another transport arrives," Helene mumbled as I walked past her, just loud enough so I could hear her over the whirring of the dozens of sewing machines.

I didn't look at her or stop on my way to deliver cut-out patterned fabric to some women at the end of the row. My eyes turned to the cold, gray sky outside the workshop window. It had been over two months since our arrival in Ravensbrück, I estimated. Some prisoners kept an immaculate track of time, but I found it foolish. It just made things harder. Time might have been important in the outside world, but in the camp, time had lost its value. It was best not to pay attention to it.

I looked over my shoulder at Helene. Our eyes met. I knew what she was hoping for with the arrival of each new transport. From what we'd learned, most German Jews were now shipped off to the East, so the chances were slim that Mother, Aunt Irene, Alice, and Ruth would come here should they be deported. But Helene and I held out hope. Nevertheless, with each day, our hopes of ever seeing our family again sank. And rumors were flying that Jewish prisoners would soon be sent from Ravensbrück to the East as well.

People had whispered about a place called Auschwitz. Somewhere in Poland. None of us had ever heard of it before. But it was whispered that many were being deported there. I wondered if it was like the place to which Bobe and Zayde had been sent. The thought made me shudder. I couldn't imagine it getting any worse than what we saw, heard, and experienced in Ravensbrück. But I'd also learned to never underestimate the Nazis' cruelty and hate for my kind.

When we left the textile workshop in the late evening that day, exhausted and cold but in anticipation of the watery soup that would take the edge off our hunger to only cause us diarrhea, we spotted a column of new arrivals come up the road. I barely lifted my eyes. Hundreds arrived daily. But out of the corner of my eye, I saw Helene crane her neck—and suddenly she grabbed my arm.

In horror, I looked for the guard. I was in no mood for a beating. I shook off Helene's grasp and moved a little away from her.

The guard hadn't noticed. Thank goodness.

"Sara!" She hissed.

"What are you—"

"Look! It's them," Helene breathed.

I stared at the column of fresh prisoners, some of whom looked around wildly, others dazed.

My mouth fell open. I wanted to scream but knew better. I reached for Helene's hand and squeezed it tightly, no longer caring about the guard.

There they walked. Mother, Aunt Irene, Alice, and little Ruth, looking around anxiously and shivering in the silently falling snow.

CHAPTER 8

1943

Because my family were all seamstresses, we were fortunate that we were all housed in our block which was already bursting at the seams. We didn't mind. I hadn't felt any happiness in a while, but with most of my family back together, I caught myself smiling again. Most of all, I was happy to see that Ruth wouldn't be separated from us. She had to stay alone in our barracks while we worked, and she had to stand for hours at *Appell* with us, but at least they hadn't taken her away.

While her being alone for prolonged periods of time worried us all, we were glad that she was with three other children to keep her company in our block. But every morning, Alice sat her down and made her promise to stay hidden within the barracks and to never venture outside. And every night, when we returned, we felt great relief when she greeted us in one of our bunk beds.

We had been together at Ravensbrück for only a week when rumors of transports to the East began to increase. One early morning, while standing at *Appell* in the freezing cold, two SS officers came to inspect us, as usual. We were told that they had to make room for new arrivals and that some of us would be sent to another camp. I looked around as panic settled over rows of women at attention. The SS officers noticed the shift in mood and shouted dismissively that better conditions, good work, and food would await us at the other camp. After all, the Reich needed skilled workers more than ever.

I wanted to believe them, but I knew better. Rumors about these "black transports," as prisoners called them, would take us East—and the East meant death. Just like what had happened to Bobe and Zayde.

Luckily, my family was not selected for transport. Only half of the women returned to the textile workshop that day. The half-empty workshop seemed eerie, and the hushed silence that had fallen over those of us who'd come back to the sewing stations was even felt by the SS officer behind the window glass. He usually ignored us for the most part, but that day, he constantly let his gaze run across the big room. He even came out twice to walk among the half-empty rows of sewing machines.

When he returned to his desk behind the glass, he slammed the door, making some of us jump. Was he angry that he'd lost half his workers, or did he fear losing more?

A week later, most workstations were occupied by new inmates, and the SS officer returned to ignoring us. Alice had joined our little team of *Anweisers* since we'd lost two to the black transport. Her extraordinary sewing skills impressed immediately.

One evening, when we cleaned up the floor around the big worktable in the back of the shop, Alice stuffed scraps of fabric in her uniform pants.

"What are you doing?" I hissed, looking around anxiously to ensure none of the guards had seen her. They didn't look our way.

"Pick some up, too. Come on."

I looked around again. One of the *Anweisers* had overheard our exchange. "What are you doing? You're getting us all in trouble!"

"Hush," I said and started stuffing some fabric scraps inside my uniform sleeves.

"Stop! Or I'll report you!"

Out of the corner of my eye, I saw a guard approaching us. We'd caught her attention. "Don't you dare report us," I hissed. We were still out of the guard's earshot.

"What's going on back there?" The guard yelled in our direction while marching toward us.

"Just finishing the clean-up," Alice said, sounding confident and assertive. The guard had reached us and looked us each in the face. Her scrutinizing gaze made me keenly aware of the fabric inside my sleeves.

"Hurry up, you lot," she yelled as she turned around and strode away again.

We all breathed out a sigh of relief. I shot the other *Anweiser* a warning look.

That night, Alice and I admired the pile of fabric in our bunk bed. "What is it for?" I asked.

"To make a doll for Ruth." She looked at her daughter, who was curled up under a blanket and deeply asleep.

I smiled. "You'll need some thread and needle."

Alice pulled both out of the breast pocket of her uniform. "Will this do?"

"How did you—?"

Alice shrugged and looked at me, full of glee. "Will you help me make it?"

"Of course! When do we start?" Alice's face suddenly turned somber. "What is it, Alice?" The expression on her face concerned me.

Alice opened her mouth, but she hesitated. With a look at Ruth, she finally said matter-of-factly, "I'm pregnant."

"No!" I yelped but immediately covered my mouth with my hands. "No, no, no. How can that be?" I said more quietly. It had been over three months since Hershel's arrest. *And how irresponsible,* I thought angrily, though shame immediately replaced my frustration. I leaned in and hugged her.

"It wasn't planned," she said unnecessarily while we held one another. Her voice trembled with fear.

Mother in the neighboring bed had heard us. She climbed over, and I let go of Alice. She put her arm around her oldest daughter, who crumpled against her chest, wetting Mother's shoulders with her sobs. Our mother stroked her head as she did when Alice was little.

Someone tugged on my sleeve and I turned around. Helene was staring at me with concerned eyes from the neighboring bunk. I looked away.

I knew what she was thinking. I had the same thoughts.

———

At the next *Appell*, we were selected for transport. My gut dropped. I thought we would be safe. We were the best seamstresses in the textile workshop, and they knew it. I was only glad that we were all being deported together.

We were marched off to the platform immediately.

Mother, Aunt Irene, Helene, Alice, Ruth, and I huddled together, shivering on the drafty train platform. The head of Ruth's ragdoll peeked out from underneath her jacket. I stuffed it in further. An icy drizzle filled the air. I'd never been colder. My teeth were chattering, and I wasn't sure if it was because of the cold or fear. Probably both.

I peered at the worn-out and frozen faces of the women in my family and said a silent prayer of gratitude that we had managed to survive together this long. And as long as we remained together, we could help each other get through it all.

I glanced over my shoulder. I had never seen a train platform so overcrowded. We were engulfed by engine steam that was spat onto those waiting to be told to get into the waiting cattle cars. Surprisingly, everything was very orderly. No chaos, just an eerie hushed silence hung over us, much like the engine steam.

There was no violence, shouting, or pushing. We all just waited, cold, hungry, and despondent.

I felt the resignation I saw in the hollow faces of those already lined up. The female guards told us that we were being relocated to another camp further east where they needed our skills. And those guards were coming with us, but that was not of any comfort. After months in Ravensbrück, I'd seen it all. Women dying from starvation, beatings, illness, cold, or taking a bullet to the head. Nothing surprised me anymore.

"Get in line. *Los*! *Los*!" a guard screamed at us while making her way through the rest of the crowd that hadn't formed lines yet.

We'd learned how to fall in line. Within a couple of minutes, the entire platform was neatly structured in rows of women lined up in front of each cattle car.

I looked up into the dark void of the car in front of us. I knew what was coming. The darkness that would engulf us, the wailing of fellow passengers, the crowdedness, the hunger, thirst, and cold.

One by one, we were pushed up and into the gaping abyss. When our car was full, the door was pulled shut with a loud crash and locked. We stood in hushed silence in the dark. Only the muffled hissing sounds from the train's engine reminded us occasionally to take a breath we were collectively holding.

Other bodies shivered close to me. Searching for my mother's arms, I found Helene's, who pulled me closer to her. Ruth's whimpering and Alice's vain attempts at comforting her brought an odd sense of relief.

A whistle screeched and the train jolted into motion. We began our journey east.

I was close to the door and through the slats, I saw the platform pass by, then houses and trees, faster and faster. But it wasn't fast enough as we would soon find out.

———————

"Wake up, Sara. Come on! Wake up!" Helene shook my shoulder. The rhythmic movement of the train had put me to sleep, standing up and leaning against the door. I had never known humans were capable of sleeping entirely upright.

The train had stopped. I tried to make out Helene's face in the dark. After a while, I could see hers and Mother's next to each other in front of me. They seemed even more haggard in the darkness.

"What's wrong? Why have we stopped?" I asked. An odd, almost sour scent hung in the air.

"Alice," Mother said. "She's sick."

"She hasn't stopped vomiting, and the train hasn't moved in a while," Helene added. That explained the unbearable smell. "Can you switch places with her? She can't stand up any longer. Maybe she can lean against the door as you have, or maybe we can manage to have her sit down by the door."

I nodded, followed by a quick, "Of course."

Helene's voice pierced the silence. She ordered everyone to push to the left to create a few centimeters of more space so Alice could move to where I stood. There was enough authority in her voice, everyone complied without complaint.

Supporting arms led Alice to where I stood. I couldn't see them, but I assumed Aunt Irene was now taking care of Ruth. When Alice appeared in front of me, I hugged her and turned us 180 degrees so she would end up with her back to the door. I took her by the hands and helped to lower her to the floor. As soon as she sat down, she leaned her head against the slats and closed her eyes.

Half an hour later, the train started to move again. Alice remained in that same position until the next day. We let her be and were just glad she'd stopped vomiting. There were a few times she'd dry heaved, but her stomach had nothing left to give.

On the second day of our journey, the train stopped several times. Sometimes for hours on end, it seemed. Alice came to it in the afternoon and began to beg for water. She wasn't the only one in our train car. Young girls and women alike began to moan for water, too. Those moans would later turn to cries.

I could no longer distinguish Ruth's whimpering in the sea of wails. I pressed my hands against my ears to drown out the suffering. My mouth and throat were parched. I was so hungry. And I'd fallen silent to conserve any shred of energy I had left. I no longer saw or sought out anyone around me. I no longer felt the cold. All of me was numb.

Late that night, the train came to another jerking stop, but this time, the door slid open, and stark lighting from what looked like a platform fell on us to reveal a gruesome scene.

Among us, in our car, were dead bodies.

The guards barked orders at us to take the dead out of the car. Weak as we were, it took at least six of us to carry one body down onto the platform. We moved at a glacial pace. We were used to death but seeing five bodies lined up, women we'd known at Ravensbrück, made us grateful we'd survived the grueling journey.

We had to help Alice down the ramp, she was so weak. Once on the platform, she steadied herself and reached for Ruth, who was led down by Aunt Irene. Alice hugged her so tightly that Ruth struggled for air and had to push back.

I looked around. A sign told me we'd arrived at Auschwitz.

So the rumors had been true.

SS guards, with German shepherds at their side, came over to us, yelling to fall in line. We complied. I looked around for our female guards who had come with us in nice passenger cars, but I didn't see them.

From the end of the platform, a man in an SS uniform with a white lab coat on top appeared. He slowly went down the lines, inspecting each one of us very briefly in almost a gentle manner. He asked Aunt Irene to open her mouth, and she showed him her teeth. He didn't care to look at the rest of us. He briefly stroked Ruth's head before moving on to the women behind us.

When he was finished with his inspection, he nodded at the female guards who had suddenly appeared.

They came among us like wolves, tearing people apart, separating the young and old from the rest of us. Yelling, they pushed Mother and Aunt Irene away from us. Mother stumbled to the ground. Aunt Irene pulled her up. Thick blood was seeping out of Mother's knee. I wanted to get over to them, but a guard yanked me back on my hair.

They attempted to rip Ruth away from Alice. Ruth screamed and kicked like a wild animal. The guard shouted obscenities and pushed Alice and Ruth in our mother's direction. "Go with them, then!"

Alice pulled Ruth with her through the surrounding chaos and mayhem toward Mother and Aunt Irene. Mother limped toward them. She hugged Alice and said something in her ear. Alice froze. Then she vehemently shook her head. Mother gently pulled Ruth off Alice, whispering something to her. Alice just stood there. Our mother hugged her oldest daughter and pushed her back toward us.

Helene darted forward and grabbed Alice's hand, pulling her to our side. The three of us watched as Mother, Aunt Irene, and Ruth disappeared into the crowd. Helene and I struggled to hold back a wailing Alice, who tried to go after them.

That was the last time we ever saw them.

Helene, Alice, and I had no time to process what happened. The guards made us run. And we ran. Like mad women. Our group came to a stop in front of a barracks where we were told we'd take showers. But that wasn't all that happened inside the barracks. They sheared off our hair and tattooed our forearms.

I barely felt it. I was numb. But I believe Alice was worse. Helene and I had to make sure that she did as she was told. We had to constantly pull her with us and steady her. Alice's eyes didn't show the terror the rest of us felt; they were empty. Dead. It scared me more than the guards or what lay before us.

Helene and I had to help Alice get dressed after the shower. Then they took us to another barracks where we would be housed. On the way in, a brown liquid and some bread were distributed. Alice didn't take any, and I spat out the brown sludge as soon as I tasted it. I was so thirsty, but I couldn't bring myself to drink it.

My sisters and I took a bunk together, and the three of us fell into an exhausted but restless sleep for whatever was left of the night.

After what felt like only a few minutes, I woke from my shivers from the cold and Alice's sobs.

She felt it all now. *That's good,* I thought. Only later would I find out that it was best not to feel.

I pulled Alice closer to comfort her and to warm us both. I fought to fall back to sleep.

After what seemed again like only minutes, guards and the *Kapo* assigned to us came in, shouting at us to get up. Dazed and disoriented, I fell out of the bed, onto the hard floor, landing on my knees and hands. A kick to my stomach took my breath away. Helene helped me scramble to my feet as I gasped for air.

We were driven out of the barracks and into a square for *Appell.* We stood for what seemed like hours in the cold lined up until an SS officer appeared. His voice was soft, but his tone was unmistakably full of hate and disgust for us.

"You will be assigned to a work detail according to your skills. You will stay with your work detail at all times. You will do as you're told and work hard, or I'll shoot you myself," he said with a nod to the female guards, who stepped forward with clipboards in hand.

"We need to stay together, no matter what," Helene said from behind me.

I nodded and looked at Alice in front of me. She stood with her shoulders and head hanging down. "Alice!" I hissed as softly as I could. "Alice, we need to stay together."

She didn't react, but I expected no less.

Eventually, a guard stepped up to our line, which meant she would get to Alice first. I held my breath, praying she would respond.

The guard turned to Alice, and to my surprise and relief, she stretched out her arm so the guard could note down her number. "Skill?" The woman in uniform barked.

"I'm a trained seamstress and dressmaker." Alice straightened her shoulders. I stared at her back. "I can sew. Whatever you need." She looked the guard straight in the eye and added, "So can my sisters, who are right behind me. We are all very skilled seamstresses."

I exhaled. Relief washed over me. My sister had returned to us. And she was trying to save us. I wanted to hug her, but I knew better and stayed rooted in my place in line.

The guard noted Helene's and my number and our profession, then moved on to the woman behind Helene. I hoped we would end up in the same work detail again as in Ravensbrück.

After what seemed like another hour in the cold, prisoners' numbers were called. Woman after woman left in groups but Alice, Helene, and I still stood in the freezing weather, waiting for ours to be called. When I dared to look around, only my sisters and I, as well as another woman, were left waiting.

Out of the corner of my eye, a female prisoner in uniform and a white headscarf and apron hurried toward us. She came to a halt at a safe distance from the SS officer. He barked at her for being late but proceeded to call four more numbers, ours and the only other woman still present. We were ordered to follow the female prisoner, who had come to pick us up. She didn't speak and silently led us toward a building on the outskirts of the camp.

We walked past barracks and chimneys. The ashes spewed from the chimneys mixed with the snow and turned the frozen ground into a gray-brownish mush. The old shoes I was wearing were soaked.

When we arrived at our destination, our guide whispered that it was the camp's headquarters. We looked at each other fearfully, but we had no choice but to follow her inside. She led us in and down the stairs to the basement.

A familiar whir reached us. We were approaching a sewing workshop.

The woman opened the door, and the familiar sound was joined by a familiar sight. Big wooden tables full of the finest fabric and tissue paper of cut-out patterns, needles, scissors, thread, and other tools. A handful of sewing machines as well. One look at Alice and Helene told me that they felt the same relief I did.

Though while the whirring of machines brought comfort, it also tugged at a still sensitive wound, one that would never heal. I thought of Mother and Father, little Ruth, and Aunt Irene. Our loss stung, and I struggled to breathe.

I followed Alice's gaze, which was locked upon a stack of fashion magazines on one of the tables. How odd I thought. I looked at the women who worked at the tables. They were sewing what looked like fancy dresses to me.

The workshop was very different from the textile one at Ravensbrück. There weren't rows upon rows of stations. The room was small and looked more like a fashion design atelier than a sewing workshop. I estimated about a couple of dozen women prisoners, all wearing white headscarves and aprons, manning the machines, cutting out patterns, pressing dresses, or sewing by hand, either standing up or sitting at one of the worktables.

The four of us were left standing at the entrance of the workshop until a prisoner in a white apron and headscarf came over to greet us. "Welcome to the Auschwitz fashion salon," she said. We stared at her in disbelief. "I'm the—" She froze. She stared at someone behind us.

We turned around and looked at the woman who'd just entered the room. She wore a fine woolen winter coat trimmed with fur. Her gloves had the same fur edge. A beautiful blue dress peeked out from underneath her hem.

The woman introduced herself as the camp commander's wife. While she seemed cold, aloof, and distant, she also spoke to us in a professional manner that made us forget for a minute that we were prisoners and slave laborers.

She took her gloves off and looked at the four of us. "You're here because I need you," she began. We stared in stiff silence. "You are here because you're seamstresses. Dressmakers. I will provide you with the finest fabrics and designs." She gestured toward the pile on one of the tables. "And you will sew the greatest fashions, the most beautiful dresses." I looked at Alice. Her brows were furrowed, though her mouth was gaping open. "In return, you'll receive bigger rations, and you will be treated justly."

Justly? It took some effort to stifle the bubble of laughter and disdain in my chest. I quietly cleared my throat.

"I assume you have sewn some fashionable dresses before?" She looked at us with raised eyebrows.

Alice nodded. "My sisters and I have." She pointed at Helene and me.

The commander's wife nodded in satisfaction. "You go over to Marta, then." A female guard, who had entered together with the commander's wife, pushed us toward the woman who had greeted us earlier. She nodded and motioned for us to sit. We did and waited for further instructions.

Relief rested on my sisters' faces. We would be safe in the workshop, in the "fashion salon," I corrected myself, and we would be able to do what we were trained to do. Together. And even better, we'd make beautiful clothes instead of uniforms for war. Something Alice had always wanted to do.

But here? In Auschwitz?

I shook my head at the grotesqueness. We were prisoners. Threatened with death every day. Nothing more. But what Father and Mother had taught us would perhaps save our lives. I only hoped that Mother, Aunt Irene, and Ruth were safe somewhere, but the haunting feeling that they were no longer alive had been following me since marching past the chimneys.

Behind Alice's back, Helene and I had discussed how only the older and sick women and children had been in the group that Mother and Aunt Irene had been ordered to join. Where had they brought them?

I pushed the next thought about Ruth away and stared at the sewing machine on the table nearest to me. It was old but familiar.

"Aunt Irene's machine," Alice whispered next to me. I nodded ever so slightly in response, but the guard had seen our exchange.

"Quiet!" the woman shouted in our direction.

We lowered our heads in anticipation of some whipping, but it didn't come.

The commander's wife held up her hand. She looked at us, then the rest of the women present. "As I said before, you all have been selected to become my seamstresses. You have the honor to sew the most beautiful dresses in the Reich. For me, my girls, my friends, and the wives of many dignitaries. You'll be working with the finest fabric and creating the greatest fashion of our time." She stopped. Perhaps because of our confused expressions, but she drew in a deep breath and proceeded, moving beyond our thinly veiled but silent reactions. "You will receive special treatment since you'll be working for me. You will enjoy other privileges and freedoms no other prisoners have. You'll be *my* seamstresses, and no one can touch you. You are under my personal protection. Do you understand?" She paused again and turned toward the three of us. "You'll start tomorrow." With a nod at Marta, she turned on her heel and walked out of the room.

The guard's glowering gaze followed her out the door, but once the commander's wife had disappeared, she turned to us. "Get up, you lot. To your barracks."

―――――

We were in the basement of the camp's headquarters from early morning to evening, for twelve hours each day. In the evening, our backs ached, and our fingers were stiff, the tips numb. I'd never sewn by hand that many hours at once. It also didn't help that the room was unheated and terribly cold, but I reminded myself daily that I could be working outside in the elements and not inside, doing what I loved.

Spring came. And so did the rain. The frozen ground slowly began to thaw and turned the whole camp into an impassable sea of mud, which clung to our shoes like lead and was dragged into our barracks and beds. But not into the fashion salon. We had to hose and dry off our shoes before we were allowed in. And once inside, we had to stop at a little sink to wash our hands and put on a white nurse's apron before we were allowed to make dresses.

It was soon discovered that Alice had a special talent for designing and creating patterns. She no longer sewed with us but rather worked on patterns, cutting them out for us to sew. She was assigned to work right alongside the lead seamstress at the personal request of the commander's wife.

One day I watched Alice leaning against the big table, directing two other girls. My eyes fell to her stomach. She was starting to show. The apron certainly didn't conceal her situation. I shuddered at the thought of the next *Appell*. She looked so frail, making her protruding belly even more noticeable. She might have gotten away with it beforehand because many prisoners suffered from bloated stomachs due to dysentery. Her ill-fitted, oversized uniform jacket had been doing its job and had been able to hide her growing belly, but the apron was too tight.

She was on borrowed time. We had to find a solution soon. A way to hide her pregnancy or perhaps a way to hide her. But the commander's wife would notice the absence of one of her most talented seamstresses eventually, when she came in for a fitting, and would certainly inquire about her whereabouts.

A shocking thought started to form in my mind. Maybe it was the commander's wife who could help? She appreciated Alice's talent. And we were under her protection, after all. She'd said so.

No matter what, we had to come up with a plan. I'd talk to Helene first before approaching and worrying Alice, who was already hanging on by a thread.

That same day, I asked Helene to come to the latrines with me in the evening. She didn't question my request since it was always best to avoid going alone. We silently made our way in the drizzle to the building where the stench was so strong that one tried to avoid breathing through the nose. Though even if I did accidentally, I would barely notice anymore.

Helene sat down next to me, and for a few minutes, we said nothing. After a while, Helene interrupted the thoughtful stillness.

"I need to tell you something." I looked at her in surprise. Her back was hunched, and she was leaning forward, resting her elbows on her thighs. When she sat back up, she pulled her headscarf off. Some of her hair had started to grow back in patches. "We need to get out of here, Sara. And if only for Alice's sake," she said, looking at me. I'd seen that determination in her eyes many times before.

"What do you mean? How could we possibly get out of here? It's impossible. You know that." I was flabbergasted at her irrational suggestion and annoyed with her pointless wishful thinking.

"I heard of some men, *Sonderkommando*, who are planning a revolt. They say they have explosives."

I stared at her. "What? What are you saying? Where would they get these explosives, Helene? Come on. These are probably just rumors, nothing more."

"I doubt it's just rumors, but I'll find out more. We can't just sit back and do nothing" She got up and adjusted her uniform before scratching her head profusely. She let out a moan of relief before putting her headscarf back on. We all suffered from lice, and the constant itch could drive one mad.

"We're not just sitting back," I said. "We work. All day. Every day. My hands are sore. I hate sewing now, Helene."

"You do? Me too." Helene sighed. The momentary defeat lasted only a moment before her fierceness showed through again. "We need to find a way to get out of here." She turned to leave.

"Don't leave yet," I said, getting up as well. "We need to talk about Alice. Haven't you noticed? She's showing, Helene. We can't wait for some undetermined escape opportunity. And besides, that would be way too dangerous. Especially for Alice, in her state."

"I don't want to just escape. I want to fight," Helene said, pushing out her lower jaw. But then she softened. "I know we need to think of Alice, though. I noticed her belly too. What do you suggest?"

I told Helene of my idea to perhaps ask the commander's wife for help. At the latter, Helene broke out into bitter laughter. "She'd probably shoot Alice herself if we told her. You're crazy to think she'd help."

"Then what do you suggest? Hide her? Where? And how? They'd notice if she wouldn't report for work.

"I don't know, Sara," Helene said, throwing up her hands. She began to walk back toward the exit of the building, and I followed her silently. Dawn would come soon, and we needed to get a little more rest out of whatever hours we had left of the night.

Once we exited the latrines, I looked to the right, at the infirmary. I stopped short. That was it!

I lunged forward and grabbed Helene's shoulder. I swung her around before she could protest. She nervously looked around to check if anyone had seen us, if some *Kapo* was around to beat us back to our barracks with her baton. Luckily, no one was in sight. "I have a plan." I motioned to the infirmary.

"You do?" Helene asked, sounding tired but surprised. She looked around again. "Not here. Back to the latrines." I reluctantly followed. I was so tired, but I had to share my proposition with her. We couldn't risk Alice or others hearing my scheme back in the barracks.

Helene led the way back inside the building and pulled me around the corner. "So?"

I looked around but saw no one. The latrines could be busy at night. For obvious reasons and others. Prisoners often suffered from dysentery and had to go several times during the night. Or they came for privacy, alone or in company. But no one was with us. We were safe from any eavesdropping.

"The infirmary," I began. Helene's eyes narrowed, but she shrugged as if she was saying, *What about the infirmary?* So I continued. "Alice could complain of an ailment or an injury and ask to go to the infirmary. She could stay there, develop an infection, and then die."

"Die? What? What are you saying?" Helene was horrified.

I grabbed my sister by her shoulders. "She could fake her own death. And then we hide her," I whispered.

Helene snorted and pulled back from my grasp. "That's your plan? That's ludicrous."

"We could also talk to the commander's wife if you think that's a better idea," I said, folding my arms defiantly. "Helene, this is the better option, you know that."

"I know," Helene said. She looked so defeated and sad. She was becoming less and less of the eternal optimist and feisty person my sister had always been. She seemed a fragment of the girl I'd grown up with. Or perhaps she appeared that way because of her now hollow cheeks and blotchy and pale skin. She'd lost her beautiful complexion, her lips were cracked and crowned with sores. Her dirty uniform hung on her thin frame like a death shroud. Though I was sure I didn't look much different.

A woman in our barracks had once offered me her shard of mirror glass. She didn't reveal how she'd gotten it, and I'd refused her offer. I didn't want to look at myself. I didn't want to know. Too scared of what would stare back at me. I'd asked why she kept it, why she wanted to look at herself, and if it wasn't better not to. But she hadn't kept it for vanity. She'd kept it so she could slit her wrists if she had to.

I hadn't seen her in weeks and wondered what had become of her.

I shook my head to disperse the dark thoughts and focused on Helene, who was standing across from me, waiting. How our roles had reversed. My always rebellious older sister who had never shunned a fight had become withdrawn and, to a point, muted. She'd always been the leader among us, but now, she let me take on that role without any resistance.

"Helene," I said gently, "let's talk to Alice and see what she thinks of that plan. Ultimately, she needs to agree."

Helene nodded. "Take her to the latrines tomorrow night and ask her," she said. I gave a satisfied nod, and we went back to the barracks where the *Kapo* greeted us with a grim face. I quickly pointed to my belly and grimaced, and she pushed us toward our bunk where Alice slept soundly.

The next night, I told Alice about the plan. She was more shocked about the fact we noticed her belly protruding than my proposition of faking her death. But she inquired about the details of the plan, what ailment or injury she'd pretend to suffer from, and where she would be hiding. I didn't have all the details but offered some suggestions. She pondered them but didn't like any of them. We decided to go to the infirmary the next chance we got to share our plan with the Jewish nurse, someone who was doing everything she could to make things easier whenever the opportunity presented itself.

When Alice and I managed to go to the infirmary two days later and told the nurse of our plan, she looked at us wide-eyed. The fear was written on her face, but once she recovered, she pulled us into the morgue where bodies were stacked to be picked up for the crematoria.

She cleared her throat. "Alice could stab or cut her hand with a pair of scissors at the salon. Make it look like an accident, of course." I drew in a sharp breath, but Alice motioned for her to continue. "She'd be sent here to get treatment. I'd try to convince them to let her stay for a couple of days. She'd develop an infection, and one week later, she'd die of blood poisoning."

"Where will you hide me after?" Alice asked.

The nurse looked around. "In here."

"What do you mean?" I tried to keep the bile down that was slowly rising up my throat.

"Underneath the corpses." She paused. "As one of the corpses."

Alice made a sound that told me she was about to vomit. I felt the same. A horror I'd never felt crept up from deep within and engulfed me, taking my air and making me feel as if I was suffocating. "Aren't they—aren't the dead," I had to swallow hard, "sent to the crematoria ever so often?" I could barely bring the words out. I looked at Alice. The horror in my gut stared back at me. I tore my eyes away and looked at the nurse again, trying to muster some courage. "How ... how would that keep Alice safe?"

"We could put her in one of the sick beds while the bodies are being removed. Just for that little bit of time. And once they're done, she can go back in there as the first corpse of the day."

I swallowed hard once more and glanced at Alice, who looked rather sick. She reached out to me to keep steady. I took her hand, then her arm for my own sake as well.

"I wouldn't know where else to hide her," the nurse said quietly with what sounded like resignation.

"And after the delivery of the baby?" I asked, ignoring Alice digging her fingers into my arm. I didn't want to hear the answer but had to ask it anyway. If the plan was supposed to work, we needed to know all the details, no matter how horrible.

The nurse looked at the corpses behind us. Alice shook her head vehemently, but the nurse shrugged her shoulders. I chewed my lower lip and only stopped when I tasted blood. I shuddered, the dead all too present in my mind, despite no longer peering at them. I wanted to run out of there and began moving toward the exit, pulling Alice with me.

"You know—" The nurse suddenly said.

I stopped and turned to her, making sure to blur my vision to avoid looking at the dead. "Yes?" I asked. Maybe she had a better idea. I prayed she would.

"I could talk to the Jewish doctor. She visits the barracks and performs abortions there during the night if needed." We looked at the nurse, shocked. She stepped closer to Alice and continued relentlessly. "If they find out you're pregnant, they'll send you to the gas. At least she'd save you."

I shot Alice a side glance. I knew my sister. I knew her answer.

Alice's lips were pressed together, and her face looked hard. She gave the nurse a silent nod and we left the infirmary in defeated silence.

I tried in vain to shake the images of the bodies that were flooding my mind, swirling around in grotesque shapes that made me shudder again and again. I didn't dare to go on about it to Alice. She was clearly as shaken as me from that visit.

She grabbed my hand. For comfort, I assumed. I squeezed it tightly and only let go when our *Kapo* came into view.

At night, I told Helene about it all by the latrines. She didn't flinch at the nurse's proposition. Her face was grim, and she said she would talk to Alice. While Helene appeared unaffected by the things I told her, I was just glad I could talk to someone about the horror I'd felt. And I was glad Helene would talk to Alice about it.

Alice. I loved her. She was my big sister and one of the most wonderful and kindest people I knew.

Fear gripped me when I thought of the danger she was in. I tried to suppress it, but it was stronger than the horror I had felt back in the infirmary.

After Helene talked to Alice, we let some days pass to give her a chance to come to terms with it all and to make a decision. But she was running out of time.

And one day, time was indeed up. Alice was called to the residence of the commander's wife. While Alice and the head seamstress sometimes met with her over designs and poured over the big black order book, these meetings usually took place in our salon. Only Marta, our head seamstress and *Kapo*, had been summoned to the commander's villa before. And from what we learned, had worked for the commander's wife at the villa.

Alice would be going right into the lion's den.

Helene and I exchanged anxious glances when the guard escorted our sister out of the salon.

Alice didn't return to the workshop, but we found her in bed when we came back to the barracks in the evening. She told us about the commander's beautiful house and garden, and how strange it had felt to sit in his living room. The commander's wife had offered her coffee and cake, and they'd discussed a design until the woman had changed the topic and inquired about her pregnancy.

So, others had noticed. The commander's wife had noticed. Helene and I held our breath as Alice continued her story.

The commander's wife had offered her condolences. I snarked, and Helene snorted in disgust. Alice shushed us and continued. She said that the woman had offered her to stay on and continue to work until delivery. She needed her to fulfill orders and wouldn't tolerate being inconvenienced.

"But the SS will kill you if they find out you're pregnant," Helene said.

"She told me I'm under her personal protection." Alice seemed confident, but her eyes darkened. "They will take my baby. She said she can't tolerate any Jewish children around and that I should be grateful that I will live."

"Absolutely not!" I hissed, trying to keep my voice down.

"What choice does she have, Sara? You tell her that," Helene said, her anger reminding me all too well of the old Helene.

I looked at Alice. Tears welled in her eyes. None of us had cried in a very long time. We no longer had any tears. Nor did we have the energy to cry. Until now. I moved closer to Alice and drew her into a hug.

"Ruth," she whispered just loud enough for me to hear. I swallowed down the tears that were starting to rise up in me, too.

After a while, Alice had fallen into a restless sleep. I lowered her down and gently rested my hand on her belly before I drew the tattered, soiled blanket over her.

I felt Helene's stare and looked up.

"You know what they will do to the baby, Sara."

"Quiet," I hissed back. I didn't want to hear anymore. I put my hand on Alice's cheek. It was wet. She was crying in her sleep.

"Sara!" Helene said quietly. She seemed less angry.

"Yes?"

"What will we do now?" She asked, sounding more like Clara than herself.

"I don't know. I really don't know." I paused, trying to quiet the thoughts that overwhelmed my mind. "I don't think there's anything that we can do," I added.

There was nothing we could do. Our plan had been foiled by the commander's discovery of Alice's pregnancy. My oldest sister was completely at the mercy of her. And Alice's baby couldn't be saved.

Either way, that was the terrible reality.

I wiped the sweat off my forehead with the back of my sleeve. It was unusually hot and humid for an early summer's day. Even in the basement, the heat hung heavily in our salon. There was no relief from it, and it was only morning.

My throat was so parched, it hurt every time I swallowed. I eyed the sink where we had to wash our hands. I longed for only a few drops of that water. I glanced at the guard by the door who, in her uniform, seemed very uncomfortable, too. When she left the workshop an hour later, probably for a moment of relief, all of us bolted to the little sink, pushing each other out of the way and trying to get a handful of water to quench the worst of our thirst.

Alice had been the slowest in making her way over. When she came close, I started shoving people out of the way so she could reach the faucet. Helene helped me guard her against the throng of two dozen thirsty women. Someone who'd been on the lookout gave the signal that the guard was returning, and we scurried back to our workstations.

It was about an hour later when Alice came over to Helene and me to hand us what I assumed was another pattern. But when she rested her hand on my shoulder and dug her fingernails in, I looked up, alarmed. She grimaced in pain and bit her lower lip.

"What's wrong?" I whispered, reaching for her hand, all the while keeping an eye on the guard who was looking up and out the two small windows above, watching whoever was passing by outside.

"I—" Alice bent over and moaned.

Helene looked at me wide-eyed but got up and darted over to the head seamstress, who'd been made aware of Alice's condition long ago. She nodded and approached the guard.

When the guard reached us, she was greeted by Alice's water breaking. She snorted in disgust and ordered Helene to clean it up, then commanded me to take Alice to the infirmary.

———

I pressed my hands on Alice's mouth again to stifle yet another scream. We couldn't let any of the SS doctors take note of what was going on. I was careful not to cover Alice's nose.

The Jewish doctor instructed her to push. The nurse was guarding the door. I left my hands on Alice's mouth but withdrew them when she was between contractions and when she turned red in the face.

"I can't do it. It's too hard. It hurts too much," Alice groaned between breaths.

The doctor stroked her arm. "Yes, you can. And you will. You have no choice. So push again, Alice."

My sister threw back her head to gain momentum and catapulted forward to push before she fell back on the cot again.

"You're done," the doctor said after the last push.

I looked at her in surprise—she held up a tiny baby that hung lifelessly off her hand. "You did it," I said and wiped Alice's forehead with my sleeve, grateful to have an excuse not to look at the baby for too long. Alice's eyes were closed, and she breathed heavily.

"It's a girl," the doctor said without looking at any of us. She rubbed the baby's back. The infant began to squirm, and a tiny faint cry escaped her. Stunned, I couldn't take my eyes off her.

I had another little niece. A tiny little niece.

Memories of Ruth and knowing that the SS doctors were somewhere in the infirmary barracks stole the small amount of joy I dared have. I swallowed hard, but the knot in my throat grew, and I used every ounce of strength to suppress the tears that wanted to well up.

I searched Alice's face, wondering about her thoughts, and what she was feeling. I only found pain. And when she opened her eyes, I saw utter hopelessness.

"What will you name her?" I asked, trying to distract her and my own thoughts. But my voice broke. Alice turned to the side, not looking at me or the baby. A tear rolled down her cheek. I took her hand in mine and rubbed it gently.

"Ruth—" Alice choked out. I put my arms around her and held her tight. That's all I could do for her. We cried while the doctor handed the baby to the nurse and left. "And I can't even tell him he has another daughter," Alice finally added between sobs. We didn't know if Hershel was alive, but Alice believed he was. Somewhere. I never corrected her. "I don't want them to take my baby. Sara, don't let them take my baby." When Alice finally looked at the infant, wrapped in an old shirt, her fingers dug into my arm. "Sara, promise me they won't take my baby."

The nurse, still cradling the little one, looked at us with determination. "We need to hide her then." I looked at the nurse, confused. Babies cried. All the time. There was no way we could hide a baby's cries from the guards.

"They won't put their hands on her." Alice sat up, determined.

The nurse placed the little girl in her arms. I gently touched the little fuzz on the baby's head. It was Alice's hair color.

"You should try to see if she latches on. She's tiny but seems strong enough," the nurse said. Alice opened her dirty uniform jacket and drew her daughter close to her nipple, but the baby wouldn't latch. She seemed uninterested in what was placed before her. She just cozied up to Alice's breast and with the tiniest yawn, fell asleep.

Soon after, Alice dozed off as well.

I let them sleep. Their peaceful breaths brought me comfort.

The nurse and doctor appeared. They reached for the little girl nestled in Alice's arm. I shook my head vehemently. I wouldn't let them. The nurse placed a hand on my shoulder. "We will hide the baby."

"Where?" I asked, shaking off the nurse's hand.

"It's best if you and the mother don't know. Trust me," the doctor said, trying to reassure me.

But I didn't trust them. I didn't trust anyone in that godforsaken place. The only two people I trusted were Alice and Helene. *Helene,* I suddenly thought. I had to tell her that she'd become an aunt again. But I couldn't leave Alice and the baby. They needed my protection—but I needed Helene to help me. To keep Alice and the baby safe. And to keep the doctor's and nurse's hands off the little one.

I looked at the two women standing by. "Please. I beg you. Just for a little bit. A few hours? Can't she hold her for a few hours? Please?" Had they no shred of humanity left?

"She has two hours," the doctor said. The nurse opened her mouth in protest, but the doctor repeated, "Two hours. No more."

"Thank you," I choked out.

It was late evening already when I ran in the shadow of the buildings from the infirmary to our barracks to get Helene. I slid into our block and found her in our bunk. While many around her were already sleeping, Helene was wide awake, sitting on the bed, clearly waiting for me or any news. As soon as she saw me, I nodded and tried to smile, but it felt like a grimace. Helene climbed down quickly and followed me out of the building.

The kapo wasn't around and didn't see us leave. We carefully made our way to the infirmary.

"Alice!" I screeched when we walked in. "What are you doing?" I darted over and tried to pull her hand away. But she wouldn't budge.

She held her hand firmly down over the little mouth, the baby writhing and squirming beneath her hold.

Tears streamed down Alice's face. "I won't let them. I won't let them take her. They will kill her. Experiment on her. She can't be in this godforsaken place. She doesn't belong here." The words tumbled out of her.

I looked for Helene, but she stood frozen in place, terror written across her face. I tried again to pull Alice's hand away, but she shoved me back so hard with her other arm, I fell. I sat where I landed and hugged my legs, rocking back and forth.

Someone, I don't know who, pulled me up and led me through the few people who had silently gathered around us and pulled me out of the infirmary. I didn't resist. I didn't want to see.

Outside stood Helene. She sobbed as she took my hand and led me back to our barracks.

We didn't speak. There were no words.

The nurse told me later that they'd swiftly buried the baby behind the washhouse during the night. The SS wouldn't get her body. For Alice's sake.

After that night, Alice was never the same. She stopped talking. Worst of all, she stopped eating. The doctor and nurse kept her in the infirmary. She no longer functioned. I wondered if the commander's wife grew suspicious and impatient because her best seamstress didn't return to the workshop.

Helene and I visited whenever we could sneak away and make it to the infirmary in the evening. There, we tried to force Alice to eat by one of us holding her down while the other tried to stuff any food that we had been able to sneak in down her throat. We felt horrible doing it, but we were desperate.

After a week, we gave up. Alice had given up. She'd become a *Muselmann*. There was no light in her eyes. She looked past everything and everyone. When the nurse told us that Alice had gotten an infection, Helene and I cried. We knew what that meant in her already weakened condition.

Days later, on an evening when thunder roared, lightning lit up the sky, and torrential rains turned the camp into a muddy lake, Helene and I were able to get away to the infirmary under the cover of the storm. When we entered, shaking the rain off us, Alice's bed was occupied by someone else.

When the nurse saw us, she only shook her head.

I stumbled out of the building and into the open. The downpour had turned into a drizzle. Helene called my name, but I didn't stop. Like a drunkard, I staggered in the direction of our barracks.

Alice! My beautiful sister. My perfect sister. How could I live without her?

Helene sprinted after me. She stopped beside me, gasping for air as she grabbed my hand and pulled me with her in silence.

Back at our barracks, and still wet from the earlier downpour, I climbed into bed. Helene was right behind me. She put her arms around me. Still, neither of us spoke. Soon enough, sobs escaped my throat. Helene joined in. We held onto each other for the rest of the night.

After that darkest of nights, Helene and I never spoke of Alice, the baby, or any of our other family members again. It would kill us to think of them. To speak of them. If we let ourselves feel the loss, we wouldn't survive. How could we?

Sewing became our only solace and refuge from the horrors around us and a great distraction from the constant hunger we battled.

Only a few weeks after Alice's death, rumors started that the commander of the camp had been relieved of his duties due to his involvement with a female prisoner whom he'd impregnated.

The commander and his family would leave, disgraced. And the fashion salon would be shuttered. We were no longer needed as seamstresses and dressmakers.

What would become of us?

CHAPTER 9
1944

After the dissolution of our "fashion salon," most of the seamstresses had been lucky to be reassigned to *Kanada*, the camp's on-site warehouse facilities, where the possessions and personal effects of Europe's Jews were received, sorted, and cataloged. Only four from our group had not come with us to the greatest human effects depot known to man. To our dismay, they had been assigned to a different work detail.

While working in *Kanada* was bearable and not the kind of back-breaking labor that would significantly lower one's prospects of survival, being surrounded by the belongings of my people, the mountains of clothing, shoes, spectacles, and everything else, took its toll. Especially when one came across personal mementos that ended up being tossed onto a pile of effects difficult to categorize and catalog or when one had to sort through children's clothing.

But working on the *Kanada* commando could be advantageous in some respects. We could secure the occasional extra food we found left behind in coat pockets or luggage. Rations had become smaller and smaller with each passing week. The war was taking its toll. Food was sent to the fronts, not the camps. Hitler needed to feed his army, so it could win the war for him. But from the rumors, Hitler was beginning to lose that war. It had made me hopeful when Helene had told me. At least for a moment.

But that moment of hope was overshadowed soon enough.

I'll never forget the day I found it in a pile of children's clothing; the ragdoll Alice and I had secretly made for Ruth in Ravensbrück. I froze when its face stared back at me. The two eyes, matching stitched black crosses, the crooked mouth of yellow yarn because we didn't have any red. I frantically looked around to see if I would recognize any of the clothing. Like a madwoman, I dug around in the pile in front of me and didn't realize that I'd lost the ragdoll in the process. I looked for it all over, but I couldn't find it again.

I told myself that I must have imagined it. But I'd seen it. Clear as the day. Right in front of me. Hadn't I?

I never recovered it, and when I told Helene at night what I'd discovered, or thought I had discovered, she doubted me.

"I just hope they're alive and well somewhere," I said at the end of my account.

Helene stared at me. "Sara—" Her eyes narrowed. "You don't think they're still alive, do you?" We hadn't spoken about our family in a long time. Her mentioning them took me off guard.

"Can I not hold out hope? Why is that so wrong?"

"Don't you know where they sent them?" Helene asked gently. I could only stare at her. Of course, I knew where they'd gone. How could I not? I knew they'd been murdered. Auschwitz was a death factory. The smoke, never ceasing to rise from the chimneys, was a daily reminder. Helene went on relentlessly. "They're all dead. Murdered in the gas chambers and burnt in the ovens."

I pressed my hands on my ears. Why did she have to say it?

I clambered out of the bunk we'd been assigned after moving to a new block that housed the *Kanada* work details. Without another word to Helene, I escaped to the latrines. I'd never before gone there alone, but I couldn't stand Helene's relentlessness for another moment. How could she talk about such horrors? Why say it so matter-of-factly? How could she be so unfeeling about our loved ones? Wasn't it enough that we had to continue to stare it all in the face day and night?

Thankfully, the latrines were deserted. I sat and rested my head in my hands, the grief piercing my heart. I angrily wiped at the tears and as a distraction, focused on the resentment I felt toward Helene for being so harsh.

The latrines were a place of refuge, and I tried to savor my solitude for a few minutes. It was a rare occasion to have a moment to oneself in the camp.

Voices fluttered through the stale, stinky air. I couldn't understand individual words or who spoke, but their whispers couldn't be mistaken. I got up swiftly to leave. I was no longer alone, and I didn't want to get caught in anything, whatever it was.

But they'd heard me and caught up with me when I exited.

The *Kapo* and another woman from our barracks I'd never spoken to cornered me.

"What did you hear?"

"Nothing. I was just—" The *Kapo* pushed me back. The wall caught my fall. With the swift movement of a weasel, the *Kapo's* face was inches away from mine. She grabbed me by the collar.

"Leave her alone," someone shouted from behind me. It was Helene. "She can't give you what you want," she added. My brows furrowed, trying to make sense of what Helene had just said and what was happening. The *Kapo* let go of me and pushed me away from her and out into the open.

"Go," Helene said while staying rooted in place. She wasn't coming with me. I wanted to protest, unwilling to leave her behind and at the mercy of the *Kapo* and the other woman, but the expression on Helene's face cut me off before I could utter a word. She mouthed an angry "Go" and dismissed me with a vehement wave of her hand.

I staggered away toward the barracks. Their voices soon grew distant. I didn't dare look over my shoulder, more afraid of Helene's anger than the *Kapo's*.

Something had changed between Helene and me that night. I had no idea what and why, but my sister grew somewhat cold and distant after that encounter.

———

Summer came. And it was an exceptionally hot and humid one. We all suffered from dysentery and an incurable thirst. And how could anyone who was there that summer, who had witnessed it and survived, forget those horrible months? Scores of Hungarian Jews, disoriented, frightened, and near death from the long journey in cattle cars in the summer's heat, arrived at Auschwitz-Birkenau. Thousands. Daily. Day and night.

Very few of the new arrivals ended up in any work details. Most went where Mother, Aunt Irene, and Ruth had gone.

To our surprise, the commander and his family returned to Auschwitz. He was assigned to oversee and maneuver the quickened pace of mass murder. And with their return, the "fashion salon" reopened. We left *Kanada* and were brought back to headquarters. Many of the SS guards were happy to welcome us back. They'd missed their slave laborers whom they'd secretly employed to mend and sew for them. We'd never refused them when asked, even though it meant more work for us after we'd worked for ten to twelve hours to fulfill our daily quota. How could we have refused them? Our lives were in their hands, and they knew it.

With our return to the basement of headquarters, other changes came. To our disbelief and joy, we were allowed to dress in civilian clothes. With our watchful guard, we were sent to *Kanada* to find some dresses for ourselves. When I spotted and put on a light cotton dress with small white polka dots emblazoned on red, I felt beautiful and clean, something I hadn't experienced in a long time.

My hair had long grown back. It was usually hidden under my white headscarf and looked matted, dull, and dirty, but the dress improved my well-being. Helene, on the other hand, scoffed when she saw the dress. She refused to wear anything that was offered to us in *Kanada* and preferred to continue wearing her prison uniform. I knew why. I had to swallow the guilt. The dress I'd put on had once belonged to a young woman who'd probably ended up in a gas chamber.

Helene, however, wasn't objecting to our new accommodations. With the return to headquarters, we also left our barracks and were housed in the basement dormitories of the same building, just a few steps down from our workshop. All dressmakers slept in single beds and had sheets covering the straw mattresses, running water, and flushing toilets. The head seamstress was our *Kapo*, a kind but strict woman. Even Helene wasn't scoffing at our improved circumstances. She knew it would only help our chances of survival. Better conditions meant less disease. And improved spirits meant hope. Hope to survive our imprisonment.

At night, when sitting on our beds, we told stories. I shared the German fairy tales and the legends my Polish grandmother had told me. It helped us pass our late evenings, keep our minds sharp and occupied, and deflect from the hunger we all felt. Always felt.

One night, one of the younger women in our group asked if I could teach her German. I was perplexed, but she kept begging me, saying it would be a valuable skill to have in the camp. She believed that speaking the language would one day save her somehow. I wasn't a teacher, but I agreed reluctantly. I hoped she would soon give up.

But she didn't. Every night, she came to my bed. I taught her some words I deemed useful and made her pronounce them over and over again. I made her memorize sentences that would be helpful in the camp, nothing a teacher of German would ever teach outside. That was all I was able to do. I didn't know how to teach her, but she was so grateful and eager to learn.

One day during that summer, our lead seamstress told us that the commander's wife demanded more dressmakers for her salon. The order book was full, and there was already a wait of at least six months. Production had to be ramped up. She asked Helene if she could find her one or two more seamstresses, and against my protests, Helene accepted the task. So a guard, with Helene in tow, was sent to the trains to find more dressmakers among the new arrivals.

It was a dangerous task. Helene could be mistaken for a new arrival and caught up in the chaos. We hoped the guard would stay by her side, to make sure Helene was safe from any mistaken identity.

I insisted my sister wear her white apron over her prison uniform and the white head scarf despite the heat, so she could be easily distinguished from the new arrivals in their civilian clothing. That was the day I was glad Helene hadn't shed her prison uniform in favor of a new clean dress.

Before she sat out, I snuck in a brief hug when the guard wasn't looking. Helene had been distant with me, but she was the only family I had left. I couldn't lose her, too. It'd be too much; it would be the end of me.

Helene hadn't returned by the afternoon. With each passing hour, I grew more alarmed. I felt the anxious stolen glances of my fellow seamstresses. No one spoke. We worked in hushed silence.

When evening came, the head seamstress could no longer hide her own fears. She asked a guard to alert the commander's wife to inquire what had happened to one of her best seamstresses, but the guard just coldly dismissed her, ignoring her pleas and demands to speak to the commander's wife. It seemed the whole camp, even the guards, were on the edge.

Heat and mass murder were taking their toll.

That evening, I retired to our dormitory alone. For the first time. Helene had been with me through this ordeal from the very beginning since our arrival in Ravensbrück. I missed her presence.

For most of the night, I lay awake with my head turned toward the door in hopes Helene would walk through it at any moment.

But she didn't.

We all looked up when someone ripped open the door to the fashion salon the next morning. I hadn't slept. The sickening knot in my stomach had only grown larger and tighter with the dawn of the new day. So, when a male SS guard we'd never seen before pushed Helene inside, I thought she was an apparition. I didn't trust my eyes or my mind. Only after the others released sighs of relief around me, did it register that I wasn't imagining things.

My throat swelled, and I pushed down the well of emotions that had been triggered by the loosening of the knot in my stomach. I wanted to run over to her and give my sister a big hug, but I couldn't. Instead, I sought out her eyes, but Helene avoided looking at me. She no longer wore her apron and headscarf. She had a few scratches on her face but looked fine otherwise.

The SS guard quietly talked to the female guard stationed at our salon door, then left.

I stared at Helene, but she was still avoiding me. The head seamstress went over to her and handed her a new apron and headscarf without a word but an inquiring gaze.

We wouldn't have the opportunity to ask her what had happened until we got back to our dormitories. We had to wait till evening.

———

It was excruciating how slowly the day passed. When evening finally drew, the guard brought us down to our dorm after we'd been signaled that the workday was done. To our dismay, only one potato per prisoner was waiting for us.

I sat down next to Helene as we were eating our meager meal. I waited for her to speak, but she didn't.

"What happened?" I finally asked, no longer willing to wait. She stopped chewing, put the rest of her potato in her pocket, and glanced at me. Her face was unreadable, but her eyes looked the same as the night we found out Alice had died.

She swallowed hard before she began. "I followed the guard to the railway platform as instructed. The guard told one of the SS officers there that we'd been sent to collect two seamstresses, and if they knew of any. Of course, they didn't. It was utter chaos there. A new train had just arrived.

"Those poor Jews. All from Hungary. They didn't know what was happening. They were so disoriented. Their journey had been long. I could tell how exhausted they were. They wanted water. They constantly wanted water. It was so hot." She trailed off and looked at her lap. A tear dropped onto her hands, which she was kneading. "There were so many of them. The SS shouted and beat them. Men, women, children. Half dead from their journey."

There was shuffling around us, and I looked up. Other seamstresses had gathered close, listening intently. They also had waited all day to find out what had happened.

"So did the SS find seamstresses for you?" someone behind me asked.

Helene only shook her head. "They ordered me to go to the *Appellplatz* and wait there. Our guard took me there but then left me to go back to the platform. I waited all day, but no one came to the *Appellplatz*. Not our guard. No SS. None of the arriving Jews. I just stood there. All day. Alone. It was so hot. I could hear the wailing, the screams, and the SS shouting, but no one came. I was wondering if they'd forgotten about me until—" Helene was breathing heavily now, and I could tell she was close to tears.

I put my hand on her arm. "You can tell us the rest tomorrow if you like."

She shook her head, took a deep breath, and continued. Her voice was low and everyone around us was utterly silent so as not to miss a word. "I heard two more trains arrive that day. One more after it was dark. The Jews from that last train were all run over to the

Appellplatz. There were so many. They were told to wait there. Then more SS officers arrived.

"They told half of the Jews waiting there to get up and to run towards these flames I saw lighting up in the distance. I wondered what was happening. I didn't understand. But then came the screaming. The shots. One after another." Helene paused. I saw her swallow hard. "I think they shot them into fire pits. I could hear them. Their terrifying screams." She pressed her hands over her ears and squeezed her eyes shut.

We stood there, frozen and silent.

Helene opened her eyes and took her hands off her ears. "There was still a group of Jews left at the *Appellplatz.* The SS shouted at them to get up and started moving them but not to the fire pits. And they shouted at me, too. I was confused. I told them why I was there. I asked for our guard who had abandoned me. They didn't listen and pushed me with the group toward a building that looked like the barracks. To take showers, they told us. Two members of the *Sonderkommando* led us into the building. The SS shouted at us to get undressed. But one of the men from the *Sonderkommando* spotted me and recognized I didn't belong there.

"He asked me what I was doing there. I quickly told him. He looked around and yelled that they'd found someone that didn't belong there. A *Kapo* came, and he was told about me. I could see fear in his eyes when the commander's wife was mentioned. He clearly wasn't sure what to do with me. The *Kapo* went to one of the shouting SS who at first dismissed him but then decided to listen when the *Kapo* insistently pointed in my direction.

"The guard came over to me. He roughly pulled me outside of the building. The *Kapo* and the man who'd discovered me followed us outside, and the *Kapo* inquired what to do with me. The young man spoke up for me.

"He spoke fluent German but had an accent. He explained to the SS officer that I was one of the seamstresses that worked for the commander's wife at headquarters and that I was only there by mistake and that the commander wouldn't be happy with them if something were to happen to one of his wife's dressmakers. He sounded very convincing. He's the reason I'm still here.

"The guard brought me back to headquarters, and after talking to one of the SS officers in the administrative office, he was told to bring me down to the salon." Helene took a deep breath.

We didn't know what to say.

"I slung my arms around Helene's. I almost lost her. The reality of how close she had come to death made me winded.

"So that was the SS man that brought you over to the salon this morning?" It was our head seamstress who had interrupted the silence and spoken first. Helene nodded.

"The young man from the *Sonderkommando* saved your life," someone behind me said.

"Yes, he did," Helene sounded exhausted.

"You need to rest," I said and pulled her up and with me to her bed. I made her lie down and tucked her in.

That night, I didn't sleep in my own bed, a luxury we had all reveled in. I slipped into Helene's bed, and I didn't let go of her arm for the rest of the night. She let me.

Several times that night, I woke up startled from nearly falling off the narrow bed. Each time, I made sure I was still holding on to my sister.

———————

An SS officer's young wife was scheduled to come in for a final fitting, and we scurried around to prepare for her arrival by quickly finishing up last-minute tasks. Our lives depended on a satisfied clientele.

She came in, accompanied by the commander's wife. The lead seamstress, who was now guiding the women to the little makeshift fitting room in the back, motioned for me to come over and help. I reluctantly joined her.

Working the fittings was a thankless job. Our clientele despised us and their unveiled disgust for and treatment of us was dehumanizing. But we also knew that an unhappy client could mean being dismissed and sent to the gas. It was best to keep one's head low and not to be in direct contact with the customers. But I couldn't avoid it today.

It was supposed to be the woman's final fitting. She seemed excited. Memories from my father's tailor shop flooded my mind, memories I had long locked away because they were so painfully beautiful. The joy in my father's face when a happy and satisfied customer had left after a final fitting. It was a moment he'd always relished. But in the camp, a satisfied and happy client meant we would stay alive another day.

When our client had changed into her new evening dress, I admired her beauty in the neatly pressed gown sewn to a perfect fit. Her beautiful skin and hair and the clean and gleaming fabric of the dress stood in stark contrast to the ugliness and filth of the camp.

I must have stared too long because the head seamstress elbowed me. I handed her the pin cushion, but the woman held up her hand. We both held our breaths. "I think it's perfect, don't you think? Just perfect." She admired herself in the mirror. Her beautiful smile was tainted only by the mark of red lipstick on one of her teeth. She brushed down the skirt and swung around.

"Just lovely, my dear," the commander's wife squealed, clapping her gloved hands.

The head seamstress motioned for me to return to my station, but the woman stopped me. "I want her to carry the dress to the car for me." I looked at the head seamstress and she nodded.

The woman changed into her old wardrobe, and we wrapped up the dress. I followed the two Nazi wives out of our basement salon and up the stairs. Outside, a fine car waited for them. The driver took the dress from me and with a wave of her hand, the commander's wife dismissed me.

Before I went back inside, I glanced over my shoulder to watch them drive away. To the side, a young prisoner, maybe my age, maybe a year or two older, approached the building I was about to re-enter. He carried something under his arm. I couldn't make out what it was.

He saw me and gave me a subtle and quick wave. Did I know him? Surely not.

He quickened his pace and caught up with me in no time, right when we both entered through the door. "You're one of them," he said quietly as he passed me. I opened my mouth to inquire what he meant by that, but he was faster. "I'm Paul," he said, turning to me. Where was he from? I could hear an accent.

I studied him. His eyes were so dark, I couldn't make out his pupils. Numerous freckles danced in his face that gave him a boyish look, despite his thin build, the hollow cheeks, and the dark circles that framed his eyes.

"Sara," I replied quietly before he was out of earshot. He threw me a smile over his shoulder and headed upstairs while I went down to the basement.

That evening, when we were lying in our bed, I told Helene about the encounter and gave her the little bit of description I could muster. I could only really recall his dark eyes, smile, and freckles.

"Sounds like the man who saved me," Helene said with surprise. "He had freckles, and I guessed he was about our age or maybe a couple of years older. I'm not sure. His German was very good. I could tell he wasn't Polish. Maybe Czech or Hungarian?" She shrugged her shoulders as if the answer to her own question didn't matter.

"Maybe it's the same person ...," I said, trying to picture his face with its features. But I couldn't.

Auschwitz had taught me not to remember faces.

While we had left *Kanada* and were back to sewing in the fashion salon and at the bidding of the commander's wife, we were often sent to the warehouse facilities for clothing, fabrics, buttons, and other sewing materials. Mostly it was the clothing of the vanished that was handed to us. Fine fabric was becoming scarce, and the commander's wife knew that the Jews of Budapest had arrived in fine clothing all summer long. The clothing depots were overflowing, and the commander's wife wanted a share of all that abundance.

The head seamstress never sent Helene on any errand runs to *Kanada*. She often sent me instead. A guard always accompanied me. We'd gotten a new guard, who seemed younger than me, after Helene had been abandoned by our previous one. Word had gotten to the commander's wife, and we'd heard that the guard had been reassigned to a less favorable position within the camp.

I was glad she was gone. I'd almost lost my sister, and I blamed her alone for it.

On a brisk early autumn morning, I was sent to gather whatever furs they would let us have. I doubted that any had come in during the summer, but furs were expensive, and people might have taken their fur-lined coats along with them in their luggage.

When the new guard and I arrived at *Kanada*, I was made to wait, as was usually the case. The guard used the opportunity to fraternize with other SS while keeping an eye on me. After a while, I spotted a young man bringing an armful of coats toward me.

It was Paul. And he seemed to recognize me as well.

"Sara!" He exclaimed with a smile. I looked around to see if the guard had noticed our little exchange, but she was caught up in swapping some items with the other guards. For a moment, I wondered what she was up to, but I dismissed it. I didn't care. Auschwitz was one big black market and not only prisoners secretly bartered and traded but the SS as well. While the inmates did so to survive, the SS were opportunists who wanted to get a piece of the cake. "It's good to see you again. Don't worry. They're busy and won't notice us talking," he said, motioning toward the group of guards.

"You work in *Kanada* now?" I asked unnecessarily.

"Yes." His smile faded. "I was fortunate to get out of the *Sonderkommando* and be reassigned here."

"You must have some good connections."

"I do," he said simply without sounding as if he was bragging. We both knew that having the right connections could increase someone's prospects of survival tremendously. He draped the fur coats over my stretched-out arm. "Here you go. Give my best to the commander's wife, would you?"

I stared at him, but he gave me a quick wink. I laughed quietly. It felt good to laugh. "I'll see you soon, Sara!" He smiled and left.

I struggled with carrying the armload of coats back to the salon. The guard made no attempt to help me carry anything but drove me on impatiently. I didn't mind. For a brief moment, I felt a light-heartedness I hadn't felt in a while. How long, I didn't know. It felt like ages.

I smiled to myself when I put down the load of fur coats in front of the head seamstress.

Helene came over to me. "What do you have to smile about?" She asked.

I quickly wiped it off my face and gave Helene a simple shrug.

———

I volunteered whenever we needed to get more supplies from *Kanada*. No one suspected anything. Except my sister. Helene knew me, and the smile I came back with gave it away. At least to her.

Twice a week, the guard and I went. Paul typically was there to fulfill what had been requested by our lead seamstress. Every time, in the very few minutes we were able to share, we got to know each other a little better. He was from Hungary. He'd grown up in a village by the Romanian border. The only son of a widow. I didn't dare ask him what had happened to his mother, and he never told me, though he did speak about his uncle in Palestine. How he regretted that he hadn't stayed there when he'd visited him and his family years earlier. He'd returned to be with and take care of his mother.

I also learned in one of our brief exchanges that Paul had been a German teacher at a secondary school in the city but had lost that job when anti-Jewish laws had been passed in Hungary after the *Anschluss*. I had stupidly complimented his German at that moment. Unsurprising, he'd rejected my praise. But it felt as if he'd rejected me.

"The only thing that German was good for now was to survive this hellhole," he said. I swallowed hard at his bluntness. Germany was my homeland, and German was my mother tongue. But for him, it had turned into the murderers' tongue.

I had always considered myself German, and my father and grandfather had been proud Germans. My grandfather had fought valiantly for his fatherland in WWI and had received the Iron Cross medal for his bravery. But my homeland had turned on us and my people. Rejected me. It no longer was the Germany of my early childhood or my grandfather's fatherland he'd defended and put his life on the line for.

I hated the Nazis. For upending my life, for taking my family, and for taking my home and homeland from me. But I couldn't admit that to Paul at that moment. Instead, I defiantly told him I was teaching a fellow inmate German per her request. He was amused. At the fact that I was doing so or because of my defiant retort or something else altogether, I wasn't sure. But that stirred up my anger even more.

After that brief but maddening exchange, I made myself a promise to no longer volunteer for errand runs to *Kanada*. Paul was insufferable, and I was in no mood to interact with him again.

One night, when Helene and I were sitting quietly on our beds which were next to each other, she asked me brashly and out of the blue why I was always the one volunteering to go to *Kanada*.

"No worries. I'll no longer go," I said, avoiding answering her question directly.

"You can't stop now," she said.

"What do you mean?" I frowned.

"We'll need you to continue to go to *Kanada*."

"Why? And who is we?" What was she getting on about? I shook my head in confusion.

"Next time you go, you need to deliver a message," she said without answering my question. Helene was cagy again, which told me she was up to something. Something dangerous and pointless, I was sure.

"Helene! I'm not going to do that. What are you up to again?" I was furious.

"Shhhh. Keep your voice down," she said while glancing around to see if anyone within earshot had heard me, but most people were either quietly conversing with others or already asleep. No one seemed to take any notice of us.

"I'm not going to deliver a message. That's dangerous. Do you want me killed?" I hissed as quietly as my anger allowed. "Why would you want to endanger me or anyone for that matter?"

"Sara, we need your help."

"Who is we?" I asked again.

"You know it's best to know as little as possible. In case—" She stopped herself. At that moment, she reminded me of the old Helene, the big sister, the fearless and defiant girl whom I'd always secretly admired for her bravery. She was so very different from me but the kind of different I'd always wanted to be. With the stern tone of an older sister, she said, "I'm sorry I asked. That was wrong. I'll go to *Kanada* from now on."

"No, you won't. I will. Like I have. You won't go. Not over my dead body."

Helene stared at me.

It took me a minute to realize what I had said. "What I mean is, I will continue to go. It would raise suspicion if you suddenly went instead of me, don't you think?"

Helene pondered my argument with a grim face, but surely she knew there was some validity to what I said. "Would you be willing to deliver a message then?" she asked hesitantly.

"I don't want to, but I will if it's important."

"Very," she said, biting her lower lip.

"Then I'll do it."

Helene cocked her head to the side and studied me. Her eyes were gentle. She put her hand on mine. "You'll need to be careful. Very careful. I don't want you to—"

"I will. I promise." I tried to sound as brave as her.

"Thank you, Sara." Helene patted my hand.

"Who is this message for?" I asked.

Helene pulled her hand away. "Paul."

"What? Why him?"

"He's helping us."

"Helping with what?" I grew impatient. Why did I have to fight for every bit of information? I was the one who was risking my life to deliver the message, after all.

"As I said, it's best if you don't know. And I understand if you don't want to do it."

"I said I'll do it." I crossed my arms and swung my leg over the other, bouncing my foot up and down. It was clear my sister wouldn't offer me any more insights. I would have to ask Paul. And after all, I could read the message I was to deliver.

Helene watched me with furrowed brows, her head tilted to the side again. Her scrutinizing gaze made me swallow. "So, when will I deliver this message?" I asked, trying to escape her inquisitive eyes.

"In a week's time," she said, holding my gaze until I had to lower my own to escape its intensity. "We need to secure paper and a pencil first."

"How? Where?"

"You know Lina?"

"The inmate secretary? Who works for one of the Scharführer upstairs?"

"Yes, her." Helene seemed to get impatient with me. "She'll steal a pencil stub and some paper from one of the waste baskets upstairs and smuggle it to us next time she's being sent downstairs with his socks for mending."

"But what if she gets caught? If we get caught?" I didn't like any of this. Why put us all in danger? For what? "What message do you want to send? I don't understand. Why aren't you telling me?" My sister had never let me in on any of her secrets or activities. I was the little sister. She'd always wanted to protect me, but we were no longer children.

"Stop asking, Sara." The finality in her tone couldn't be mistaken. She exhaled a sigh and stretched out on her bed, turning her back to me.

I had no choice but to let it go. I would have to find out more another way.

So, not to raise any suspicion on anyone's part, I continued to go to *Kanada* twice a week to get supplies for the fashion salon. Paul was there each time. He happily greeted me, but I ignored his friendliness and remained tight-lipped in his presence, uttering a mere hello and goodbye. He let me be and didn't push.

The following week, he asked me if I had something for him after I had told him the order for the workshop. I nodded, barely noticeable. "It's in my sleeve," I whispered as quietly as possible, hoping to be still audible. He confirmed with a nod of his own.

The night before, when most were already deep asleep in our dormitory, including me, Helene had shaken me awake and pushed a piece of paper into my hand. While scanning the dormitory, she'd hissed to hide it in one of my sleeves. It was an easy hiding place. Unlike the wide-open sleeves of the prisoner uniforms or uniform dresses, the cinched cuffs of my polka-dotted dress allowed me to hide a lot of things without the chance of them falling out and being discovered. Still, I was keenly aware of the small paper I'd stuffed inside my sleeve. I was sure someone would notice that it was in there. It felt like hot iron against my skin.

Helene's encouraging glances didn't help dissolve the knot in my stomach that had begun to form. I wanted to read the message but didn't dare take it out after I'd stuffed it away. Perhaps I would have the chance to read it in the morning. In the washroom or by the toilets. But the chance never came.

After I had been unable to sleep for the majority of the night, I'd finally fallen asleep in the early morning hours. Helene had to shake me awake again, and I barely had the time to get ready, let alone read the message hidden in my sleeve.

I looked at Paul, who was checking to see if the guards were paying us any attention. They seemed busy talking. He drew closer to me.

Only inches away from my face, he said, "The moment I hand you the items you came for, put that paper in my hand, alright?"

I simply nodded, ignoring the knot in my stomach and my dry throat. What if I dropped it? What if we were discovered? I swallowed hard.

Before Paul withdrew, he gave me a quick peck on the cheek. I looked at him perplexed and over to the guards to see if they'd noticed. One of them looked at me with furrowed brows. My heart dropped. He'd seen us.

"Get away from him," the SS guard shouted at me. I quickly took a step back and lowered my head as the guard came toward me. He took me roughly by the arm and pulled me farther back. I looked at Paul. His face was tense.

"Get her what she needs. Come on! Get a move on," My guard approached too and shouted at Paul, then she turned to me. "Wait by the door there. And no funny business, missy. Or you'll find yourself in Birkenau tonight."

I froze. Our guard had never threatened me or any of the other seamstresses directly before. My hands started to tremble, and I pressed them against my thighs to make them stop.

It took Paul an eternity to collect the ordered materials and clothing and return with them. I barely dared to breathe. The entire time, the guards didn't take their eyes off me.

Paul finally appeared and stepped up to the counter. The guard waved me over to the counter too but thought twice of it. She took me roughly by the arm and pushed me forward. She was right by my side while I gathered up all the things Paul had laid out for me on the counter. Under her watchful eye, it was impossible to retrieve the paper from inside my sleeve and put it in Paul's hand.

It would have to happen another time. I couldn't risk it.

Paul gave me a quiet nod, and I knew he thought the same.

When the guard and I returned to the fashion salon, the lead seamstress was told what had happened and that I was never allowed to go to *Kanada* again.

Helene listened to their exchange. She looked over at me, not bothering to hide her anger.

I lowered my eyes. I'd never see Paul again. It stung harder than I expected, but maybe it was for the best. We had become less careful about our interactions. It was too dangerous. For the both of us.

The guard's threat still rang in my ears.

As soon as we were in the dormitories at the end of the workday, Helene cornered me. "Sara! How could you be so careless!" She said under her breath, but her tone was unmistakably sharp.

"I'm sorry." I was defeated and tired. I angrily wiped a tear away that had squeezed out of the corner of my eye. I was in no mood for Helene's ire and lecture. "I'm sorry I couldn't deliver your message. I'm sorry I failed. I had all the intentions of doing it."

"Why are you bashing your eyelashes at Paul?" she hissed.

"I'm not. I don't even have any!" It was true. Though I once had lush lashes my sisters had envied, they'd fallen out a long time ago.

"Sara!"

Helene grabbed me by the arm, but I shook her off. "He kissed *me* on the cheek. I didn't do anything to make him do that. Besides, all you care about is that your precious message wasn't delivered." I no longer cared if anyone heard us.

"Keep your voice down," Helene said, oddly calm suddenly. She put an arm around me. "And don't be ridiculous. I care about you, not that message, Sara. You must know that! The guard could have sent you straight to the gas or shot you on the spot! I can't lose you, too. Don't you understand?"

My gut tightened. "I do." I understood all too well.

Against the protests of the lead dressmaker, Helene insisted on being the one to be sent to *Kanada* now. In my stead. Others had volunteered, but my sister was relentless. She was fearless.

For whatever purpose she wanted that message delivered, I still didn't know. I just hoped she would be careful and that her scheme wouldn't be discovered.

———

I saw Paul again. On an early autumn afternoon. On the steps of headquarters where we first met. I was on my way in after helping one of the SS wives carry her dress, and he was leaving. He stopped in his tracks and changed directions immediately when he saw me. Without a word, he followed me inside and down the stairs. I looked around to see if anyone had seen his maneuver, but it seemed to have gone unnoticed.

I continued down to the basement, my heart beating hard against my chest. I couldn't believe he was there with me, but his footsteps and breathing so close behind me stopped me from questioning if I was seeing things.

I was surprised how much I'd missed him. The sadness that had hovered over me was evaporating and forgotten happiness cleared my head. I'd been stuck in a haze over the past week, unknowingly. But that clarity also made me keenly aware that we were being careless once again.

Why had he followed me? What if someone saw us? It was too dangerous.

The hallway in the basement leading to the fashion salon seemed deserted. I paused my steps and turned around to face him. Paul was scanning the stretch of hallway behind him. So did I. He then looked at me, smiled, and reached for my hand, but I shrunk back when he gently touched my face with the back of his hand.

"I'm just trying to wipe away the snippets of thread stuck to your cheek. Just hold on." With two gentle strokes, he wiped them away. It felt as if the wing of a bird had brushed against my cheek. I tried to ignore the flutters in my stomach. Involuntarily, I close my eyes.

His lips brushed against mine. Ever so gently.

I opened my eyes. He was looking straight at me.

"I'm sorry. I shouldn't—" He lowered his head.

I took a step back, yet again, as if I'd lost all control over my own body, I smiled. He instantaneously smiled back, and for a moment, I forgot where we were and the dangers around us.

"I better go," he said and gently squeezed my hand. I simply nodded and turned around, scanning my surroundings. There were voices from upstairs and the whirring of sewing machines farther off, but we otherwise seemed still to be alone. "I've missed you, Sara!" He said and let go of my hand. "I shall see you again soon."

I wanted to ask when and how, but he was already disappearing down the hallway, and I could hardly shout after him. Only then did I notice I was breathless, though whether it was from the encounter, Paul's smile and gentle kiss, or the danger we were putting ourselves in again, I wasn't sure.

Once Paul was gone, I proceeded to the fashion salon. Our guard sat outside the door, flipping through a fashion magazine. When she saw me, she motioned for me to come over to her. I held my breath. Did she know? Had she seen me? Paul?

She tapped on the picture of a fancy dress on one of the pages. "So, you could really make something like this?"

I nodded, relief washing over me.

The guard scooted up closer, enough that I could smell the coffee on her breath. She whispered, "I want you to make me one just like that."

I couldn't deny her, but it would mean even longer hours for me. She wasn't part of our regular clientele of SS officer wives or the commander's wife. Ordinary guards weren't allowed to place an order for a dress with us. They had to use the mending depot for any of their clothing needs.

"I'll have to speak to the lead seamstress," I said, eyeing her carefully. Her brows furrowed, so I quickly added, "I need to speak to her to see if we have all the materials needed for it. It's a very fancy dress."

"It is. That's why I like it." She slammed the magazine shut and gave me a shove toward the door of the workshop. "You go ask her then. Just know that I won't forget it if you make it for me."

I nodded and slipped inside.

Bent over the embroidery for another evening dress, my mind was racing. About the guard's request and Paul. I would speak to the lead seamstress tonight, I decided, and maybe this side order would offer me the opportunity to return to *Kanada*, if she let me. I'd be able to see Paul. The guard would certainly accompany me to get the materials for her dress and maybe allow or even ignore any interactions with Paul.

For the rest of the day, my thoughts drifted again and again to Paul's kiss. I must have replayed it a thousand times in my mind. It wasn't something that I'd expected to experience in the camp. Although I'd always tried to imagine my first kiss, it stood in such stark contrast to anything I had seen and experienced or imagined in the camp. And all I wanted now was to kiss him again. To see Paul again.

I had a purpose again.

But with every passing hour, I became gloomier. I scolded myself for my frivolous thoughts, for my feelings, for my change in focus.

I looked over to Helene, who was stitching buttonholes onto a woman's coat. She was biting her lower lip, as she often did when she was concentrating. She was the only family still with me. We needed to continue to protect each other, so we could make it out alive. Together.

At the end of our long workday, after most had left the fashion salon, I spoke to the lead seamstress about the guard's request. She wasn't happy about the extra order, but she also knew I had no choice but to oblige her.

She spoke to the guard for me to tell her that I would need to go to *Kanada* to get the needed supplies. The guard happily agreed, anxious to see her dress made. It was all going according to my plan.

I would see Paul again. But was it wise or feasible?

Only two days later, the guard marched me to *Kanada*. The chilly morning air penetrated my dress easily. I hugged myself, trying to keep warm. Winter would soon be here and in Poland, the winters were harsh and relentless, especially for the prisoners of Auschwitz-Birkenau. The death toll among inmates who'd not been selected for the gas right away but slaved away in the different work commandos rose drastically starting in November, especially for those who were exposed to the elements.

The seamstresses and all those who labored inside were better off. Working inside with more sanitary facilities and a bed and blanket to ourselves and the occasional extra rations made us privileged among the inmates and raised our chances of survival exponentially, especially during the winter months.

The guard and I arrived in *Kanada* just as the sun started peeking through the morning fog. We had to wait for a long time for Paul to appear and place our order with him. When he saw me, he broke out into a big grin. He seemed genuinely happy to see me. I hoped the guard hadn't noticed, but she was busy trying to get the clumps of dirt that had collected on the bottom of her boots off with the help of her whip.

I turned my attention to Paul, who was standing in front of me. My eyes were drawn to a big gash on the side of his head. My face fell. "What happened?" I mouthed. The wound clearly needed stitches. Had Paul gotten in trouble?

Instead of answering my question, he quickly looked over to the guard, who gave him a quick nod and turned her back to us. He stared at the guard, confused.

"She will leave us alone today," I said. He still looked confused. "I'm here on an errand run for her," I added, then I turned my attention back to that nasty wound on his head. "What happened?"

"One of the *Kapos* ... you know."

"But why?"

"It doesn't matter." He waved it away. "I'm so happy to see you here."

"Me too." I still couldn't take my eyes off that angry gash. It looked infected, too.

He placed his hand on mine and with a look at the guard's back, he inched closer and whispered, "I'll get us both out of here. I promise."

"How?" I didn't take him too seriously. There was no way to escape Auschwitz. Some had tried but only a couple of inmates had actually managed to do so if the rumors were true. And if someone got caught trying to get out, execution was the only form of punishment.

He looked at the guard again, her back still toward us. "We'll disguise ourselves." He had said it so quietly, that I wasn't sure I heard him correctly. At my puzzled expression, he added, "I'm working on a plan."

"But I can't. My sister—"

"She's in on it."

"I'm not leaving her. Never."

"She's coming with us, Sara." So, the message Helene had tried to pass on to Paul was about an escape plan?

"Are you getting the stuff she needs or not?" The guard shouted in our direction. I quickly rattled the list off to Paul, and he disappeared to get me what I needed.

After a few minutes, he came back with the materials. The guard grunted in satisfaction and motioned for me to come along. I gave Paul a quick nod. I wanted to talk to him more. Mainly to convince him that it was a crazy idea and too dangerous, but the guard had gotten what she needed and was in no mood to let me dilly-dally any longer.

———

The evening after her second official errand run to *Kanada* for more supplies for the fashion salon, Helene pushed a piece of paper into my hand while we were walking from the workshop to our dormitory at the end of the day. It was the first night since I had gotten started on the guard's dress that we walked back together. I usually stayed behind in the workshop for another couple of hours to sew. But I was exhausted and unusually tired. The extra workload was taking its toll. I needed to rest.

The texture of the paper in my hand surprised me. "I told him I didn't like this. At all. But he insisted," Helene said. "And you know ... I owe him my life."

Paul.

My heart skipped. I quickly stuffed the paper into my sleeve. I'd read it after most were asleep. So much for that much-needed rest. I was too excited to sleep anyway.

I couldn't wait until voices in the dorm had fallen silent. Not everyone found sleep during the night. And no one ever slept soundly. The nightmares of the day made their way into restless dreams at night. And with the lower temperatures that the cold weather of autumn had brought into the basement, some of the prisoners had already begun to fall ill with colds or worse.

It was of the utmost importance to stay healthy. The SS didn't tolerate disease around them. One would be immediately sent to the infirmary if found sick, and a simple cold could easily turn into something more serious.

I ignored the sniffles and the occasional cough echoing off the walls of the dormitory and pulled out the piece of paper Helene had reluctantly stuffed in my hand. I opened the neatly folded paper and let my thumb caress the small handwriting. Paul. I could tell it was written in haste. The penciled words had some smudges. But I could decipher it all regardless, and I hung onto every word.

My dearest Sara,

I have missed you. More than I would like to admit. Call it serendipity that I have found you in this hell, but you were meant to be in my life. And alive we must stay. At every cost.

One day, we will leave this place. I'm working on it. Will you trust me, Sara? One day, I will buy you flowers that you pick out and a beautiful brand-new dress no one has ever worn before. And we go on long walks to talk and have ice cream. You will see.

They are sending me again to headquarters tomorrow for a delivery. It usually happens around 15:00. Will you run into me again, Sara? On the steps? If not, meet me in the basement hallway if you can. I have to see you.

Your Paul

My eyes swam from line to line, but then I quickly folded the paper and went to the washroom. I stood in front of the toilet, unfolded the paper again, and quickly ripped it into little pieces which I dropped into the bowl. I looked over my shoulder and with a swift movement, I flushed Paul's letter, every word already imprinted in my mind.

The next day, my sole goal was to be able to meet Paul, but the lead seamstress had no finished order with which she would have sent me down the stairs to carry to someone's car. I would have to meet him in the hallway, but I needed a reason to leave the workshop and get past the guard.

Her dress! Of course!

But … I wasn't allowed to attend to her special order until after I'd fulfilled my quota for the day. I would have to ask the lead seamstress if she would make an exception. She would question my request, of that I was sure, but I couldn't think of another way. Unless ...

I kept checking the large clock on the wall. I'd chosen to ignore it from the very first day until today. Acknowledging its presence would only make the days seem longer and never-ending. The big hand was approaching the ten, and I started to cough. Repeatedly and obnoxiously. I made a grand gesture out of feeling my forehead, ensuring the lead seamstress saw me.

She came over. "Are you unwell, Sara?"

I nodded. "I don't feel so good. My throat, and now this cough. I think I'm running a fever." Out of the corner of my eye, Helene perked up. "I think I need to go to the infirmary."

The lead seamstress took in a sharp breath. "That bad?" I nodded, trying to look pained. "Are you sure you want to be sent to the infirmary? You know what that can mean ..." I nodded again.

"I'll take her." Helene had appeared beside us. The lead seamstress gave a reluctant nod. Helene lifted me up and walked me out of the room. Outside the door, the guard stood from her stool. "Where do you two think you're going?"

"Infirmary," Helene gave back. "She's very ill."

The guard immediately took a step back from us. She pulled out a white kerchief from the breast pocket of her uniform and covered her mouth and nose with it. She dismissed us with an impatient wave of her hand.

We started walking away from her, but she stopped us. We held our breaths. "But what about my dress? Who will sew my dress now?" she asked.

"I will," Helene said. The guard looked from her to me and back to her. "You're her sister, right?"

"That's right. And a much better seamstress than her, if I may add," Helene said. I stared at my sister. How could she be so forward with the guard? I swallowed.

"Now, don't be fresh, missy." The guard placed one hand on her whip and stepped toward us. "You watch yourself, you hear me?" Helene nodded obediently. A rare sight. "Alright, you'll continue with my dress then," she said. The guard waved us along, and I let Helene support me on our way down the dark hallway and around the corner where I hoped Paul would be waiting for me.

As soon as we were out of the guard's sight and earshot, Helene let go of me. "And how is this supposed to work, Sara? The infirmary? Really?" She looked angry. "And why in the world would you want to go there?"

"To meet me." Paul. He walked toward us in the dimly lit hallway.

"I see," Helene no longer looked angry but annoyed. "You're being careless again," she added, rolling her eyes.

Paul and I were silent and let Helene give us a lecture. I looked at Paul. He seemed amused and gave me a wink while Helene let us have it. I smiled at him and let out a quiet sigh. It wouldn't be just the two of us today. I sighed again. But I was glad to see Paul, nevertheless.

"Since you're here, too, Helene," he winked at me again, "we could discuss our plan."

"What plan?" I asked.

"To escape, remember?" he said quickly. Oh, that plan. Right. So he had been serious about it. But it was too dangerous! Was that the reason he had come? Had he actually wanted to see me? Or was he meeting me to discuss a futile plan? A risky undertaking that would leave us all dead?

"I don't think this is a good idea," I said. "There is no way—"

"We're trying to find a way, Sara. A way to succeed and not get killed," Helene interrupted.

"We haven't got much time." Paul was shifting impatiently. I wasn't going to be kissed today. That much was clear. But I also was reluctant to be pulled into something by those two I knew would fail.

Paul had asked me to trust him. But did I trust him with my life?

We heard steps coming down the stairs and fell silent. Holding our breaths, we pressed our backs against the wall. The steps drew nearer. Paul grabbed my hand and squeezed it gently. The steps stopped and entered a room not too far off. We gave a collective sigh, and Paul dropped my hand.

"There's a *Kapo* in *Kanada* I trust," Paul said, his eyes on the hallway. "He told me he's been sent to the SS uniform depository on occasion. I will try to accompany him next time and see if I can smuggle out some uniforms.

"That's the plan? To dress up as SS?" I was stunned.

"Disguise ourselves as SS," Helene clarified.

"You both look as German as one could," Paul said. I furrowed my brows. What did that mean? "You'll easily pass." I doubted that. We were skin and bones, but Helene's and my hair had grown back.

"I'm tall. With some additional layers of clothing from *Kanada*, I can fill out that uniform to look intimidating," Paul added. I raised my eyebrows.

"And then we just walk out of here?" I asked. That was ludicrous.

"We're still trying to work that part out," Helene explained.

"I need to go," Paul said abruptly. "It's been too long. I don't want to lose my courier privileges." I wanted to say something. Our meeting hadn't gone as intended, and disappointment washed over me. But Paul murmured, "I'll see you soon," Too quickly and was already off down the hall.

"We need to come up with an explanation for why you didn't stay at the infirmary." I stared at Helene blankly. She was biting her lower lip and looking up and down the hallway. Since I had nothing to contribute, she went on. "We'll say that the doctor released you and declared you fit to work. No fever. Just a nasty cold. Yes, that's what we'll claim."

She pulled me with her back to the workshop.

The guard would be happy to have her dressmaker back.

With autumn in full gear and the approaching winter came a wave of typhus and the rain of allied bombs. One was more welcome than the other. Both inmates and SS died or were injured in the latter.

Despite being rattled by explosions and injured friends and the planes overhead, seeing the SS scrambling for their lives made us hopeful. Maybe Hitler was losing this war. Maybe we'd be able to go home soon.

Home.

The thought of home left me with a sense of great sadness. Helene and I no longer had a home. Our family had been our home, but everyone we loved was gone. How could we ever return to Salzhausen where we'd been born and raised but our father had been brutally murdered?

What would we do after everything was over? Where would we go? *If* we survived.

It was the noise of allied bombers overhead and the destruction caused by the bombs that made me realize I'd not made any plans for the future.

But one didn't make any such plans in Auschwitz.

Neither did we make any further escape plans. Paul believed it would only be months, if not just weeks before the Allies defeated the Nazis, and we would be liberated. Helene wasn't happy that it was put on hold. She didn't want to wait and see the outcome of the war. I was just glad that we wouldn't try to escape. I didn't want to risk being captured and executed right before the end.

The warning sirens of the bombing raids were followed by another outbreak of typhus in the camp. We heard that Birkenau was hit hard. It only took a week before the first case of typhus was discovered in our workshop. We had no idea where the oldest seamstress among us had contracted it, but she was immediately sent to the infirmary.

She never returned.

Helene continued to make the occasional errand run to *Kanada* under the watchful eye of the guard whose dress I had almost finished. Helene smuggled in whatever she could from *Kanada* to strengthen our health whenever she had the chance.

Our bodies barely hung on. I couldn't remember when I'd had my last period. It seemed a lifetime ago. My hair had started to fall out as well, and the sore on the corner of my mouth didn't want to heal.

One night, my sister told me to check under my blanket, and I found an apple. I looked in surprise.

"From Paul," she said.

I took my spoon and whittled off a piece. I offered it to Helene, but she shook her head. I told her I insisted. She shook her head more vehemently.

"You need it more than me," she said.

I savored every bite. It was the most delicious food I'd had in a long time.

A week later, I woke up with a fever. I kept it from Helene and pushed through the day in hopes it would subside, but when I refused our meager ration that night and crashed onto my bed, Helene noticed.

"Sara!" She pressed the back of her hand against my forehead. Her cold palm was so soothing on my burning face.

"I know," I said weakly. When I grimaced at her, there was terror in her eyes.

"We need to get you to the infirmary," she said and tried to pull me up.

"It will be gone by tomorrow. I don't want to go there. Don't make me. Please!" I closed my eyes. I was so tired and exhausted. And entering the sick block meant being at the mercy of the SS doctors who sometimes conducted cruel experiments on sick prisoners and selected them for the gas to make room. "I just need to rest ... Let me be. Please!"

Helene left me alone after that. Her silence, however, only added to my own dread.

That night, I drifted in and out of sleep.

The next morning, I was pulled up and dragged off my bed. I never opened my eyes. I must have lost consciousness because when I woke up again, I was in a bed in the infirmary, still burning up.

I looked around. All the beds were occupied by half-dead bodies. Some breathed very heavily. Others moaned. I panicked. I didn't want to die. Not like that. Not now. Not there!

The nurse came over when she noticed I was awake. "You were out for three days straight. You got typhus, my dear." I closed my eyes. The kind Jewish nurse, an inmate just like the rest of us, put a wet rag on my forehead. "Your fever hasn't broken." She put a dark liquid to my lips, but I turned my head away. "You need fluids." She took me harshly by the chin and turned my face back toward her. Ignoring my protests, she pressed the rusty enamel cup against my lips until I opened my mouth. The liquid tasted like metal.

I swallowed hard. A moment later, I was dry-heaving violently. I tasted bile and the little bit of liquid I'd been forced to consume made its way back up. My stomach was cramping up and I winced in pain. I curled up onto my side.

In the process, the blanket had slipped off me, and out of the corner of my eye, I saw that my body was covered in a rash. I closed my eyes.

The nurse wiped the vomit off my face and put the rough blanket back on me. She rested her hand on my arm, trying to comfort me. "Your sister was here last night," she whispered. "She's trying to get you some medicine."

A tear rolled down my cheek. Helene. I was surely dying, but how could I leave her? I was all she had left. But Helene was strong, resilient, and brave. She would be able to go on without me. She would live.

An image of someone else wormed its way into my mind. Paul! His face, his smile, him winking at me. I saw his face clear as day in my mind's eye. I could remember every feature.

I continued to slip in and out of consciousness. The days passed. How many, I didn't know nor cared to know. The SS doctor appeared occasionally. Although I remembered seeing him only a few times, I was told he came daily. To determine my fate, I assumed.

One night, someone sat at my bedside. I forced myself to open my eyes. Helene. Her face was unreadable.

"Sara!" she said, her hand on my cheek. "How do you feel? Any betterment?"

I searched for her other hand and found it. I gave a weak nod. How could I tell her that there hadn't been any improvement?

"We're working on getting you some medicine. Please hang on."

"Medicine? From where? How—?"

"Sssshhhhhh." She looked around to see if anyone had heard. I doubted it. I could barely hear myself speak. "Quinine or Prontosil," she added. "Whatever we can get our hands on and will bring you relief.

"You need to get better. Do you understand, Sara? Don't give up now!" I registered the urgency in her voice, but it didn't affect me the way it might have before I'd fallen ill. I couldn't tell her that there was no hope for me.

I closed my eyes. "Be careful. Please. Helene—" The few words I had uttered had exhausted me, and I drifted off.

For how long, I didn't know. I had no concept of time.

Days ran into nights and nights turned into days. I didn't keep track, nor could I even if I had wanted to. My mind was hazy. My memories slipped. Typhus not only took its toll on my body but also on my mind.

The next time I woke up properly, I was sure I'd dreamed of Helene visiting me. But when the nurse came to my bed on her evening rounds, she whispered that she had some medicine for me. So Helene's visit hadn't been a dream? The nurse told me quietly that my sister had indeed acquired some medicine for me, but how? I assumed Paul had secured some in *Kanada*, and she had smuggled it to the sick block.

The nurse forced me to drink the same brown liquid. Unlike the last time, though, I took it willingly. It tasted bitter. Perhaps it was laced with whatever they'd been able to get.

Helene. Paul. They weren't giving up on me.

Twice a day, the nurse made me drink the same concoction. I ignored the blurred vision, dizziness, and splitting headaches that I developed over those days. Eventually, my fever broke, and I actually started to feel better. My appetite returned. I was ravenous, even. But there was no food. Only the dismal rations.

The nurse was all too aware of my blight. The blight of many typhus patients. If one was lucky enough to survive the illness, starvation took most of those who'd cheated death. Our already emaciated and disease-stricken bodies needed to recuperate but that was impossible on the meager food rations we received.

The SS doctors knew that as well. Their answer?

Selection.

After a few more days, I began to be able to sit up in my bed. I was still very weak, and my hunger was getting painful. Helene smuggled in some extra food, but it wasn't nearly enough. The temperatures had also plummeted, and the coal-fired iron stove in the center of the sick block was no match for the Polish winter. I spent the nights curled up in a fetal position to warm myself. The thin, rough blanket provided only a little protection against the harsh cold.

I constantly shivered, and the hunger pains crippled me. My thoughts were singularly occupied with food, so much so, that to my own horror, I repeatedly found myself gnawing on my blanket.

One early morning, when the weak winter sun had not yet risen, I woke up startled. Someone had pulled off my blanket. The cold engulfed me mercilessly, and I started to shiver violently. "No," I moaned, swatting at the hands that were trying to pull me out of bed.

"Sara! Cooperate! The SS doctors are coming." I froze. My eyes flew open, and I tried to focus on the faces around me. "They will give everyone here an injection. We need to get you out of here. Now!" Helene. My sister and the nurse were pulling me up and out of bed.

"Be careful!" The nurse said to her as my sister stabilized me. I hadn't stood up in weeks.

Helene put a hand on the nurse's shoulder. "Thank you for warning me!" With that, Helene dragged me with her out the door. The SS guards outside the door let us leave. Had they been bribed?

My feet barely found the ground, which shone frozen in the early morning light. I felt as if I was floating. I had no idea how Helene was able to support me like that, but I was walking. In a way. More like sliding, desperately trying to find hold with my feet while Helene pressed on, but still.

"I need you to do your best to not look so sick and weak, Sara!" She said between breaths.

A cackle escaped my mouth. My voice was failing my bitter laugh. I tried to clear my throat, but I was so out of breath and parched, even that failed. "I'm ... trying," I brought out, winded. "Where ... where are we ... going?"

"To the workshop. You're better now. You can work. You will have to work, Sara!"

"I can't."

"Yes, you can, and you will." She was relentless. "Straighten up now. Come on."

I looked ahead at our building. Upon seeing the steps and the entrance, I thought of Paul. I followed her instructions and tried to straighten my shoulders, unsure if it showed.

"Slow down, Helene."

She did.

I thought I was ready to walk on my own, and I let go of her, trying to show her I could be strong. But I almost fell when I did. She took my arm again and wrapped it around her shoulders. She held me tighter than before, and together, we walked up the stairs. Slowly but steadily. I was amazed at myself. The stairs had seemed daunting.

Twice, SS passed us, but they didn't stop us. I was sure I looked like death, but I got past them.

When we arrived at the basement workshop, our guard was in her usual spot. She barely looked at us.

"I think they know it's all going to be over soon," Helene whispered in my ear when we were inside the workshop. She led me to a chair and sat me down with a groan.

The lead seamstress came over and nodded at me. "Good to have you back, Sara!" I could only give her a nod back. I was utterly spent and tried to catch my breath. Pearls of sweat had collected on my forehead. The damp cold of the basement was almost refreshing in contrast. With her kind welcome, the lead seamstress had placed some stitching work in front of me. "Stay seated here for the rest of the day. I started this for you already. Just finish that and it shall do for today."

I gave her a nod of gratitude and took up the needle and beautiful stitched pattern. The fabric was Dupion silk and very thin for which I wouldn't need much strength to push the needle through, but my hands were shaking, and my fingertips were numb. The needlework swam in front of my eyes. It wouldn't be easy.

I searched for Helene and found her looking at me from across the room. I attempted a smile. She nodded encouragingly and turned her attention back to the laid-out patterns on the table in front of her. She then blew into her frozen fingers and picked up a pair of scissors.

Gazing at my sister, I realized I would never survive without her. She had always been the strong and brave one among all my sisters. I needed her to make it out of the camp.

At the same time, I was keenly aware that I'd become a burden to her and that my existence not only made everything more difficult for her but also endangered her life more than it already was.

I had never been more grateful for Helene, but the accompanying guilt was hard to swallow.

Fortunately, with each passing day, I improved a little more. The lead seamstress made sure my work was light and I was able to spend my long workdays in a seated position.

Helene still made the errand runs to *Kanada* and occasionally was able to smuggle back some food, not just for me but for the other seamstresses as well. Sometimes she also brought back a note from

Paul, who was glad the medicine had worked and that I was out of the infirmary. But I hadn't seen him in weeks.

I missed him and was desperate to see him. He assured me in each note that we would see each other soon, but how, I wasn't sure. And while with each passing day I grew healthier and stronger, I also grew more restless.

By the second week back in the fashion salon, I had developed a nasty cough. I tried to hide it as best as I could, especially when passing the guard, but it became more difficult by the day. Helene not only grew worried but also impatient with me, as if the cough was my own fault. Luckily, I didn't develop another fever. The dry cough was my only symptom I needed to hide.

I wasn't the only one hiding things. On several occasions, I spotted Helene and the head seamstress talk quietly. That alone was not a reason for my suspicion since Helene was her best seamstress and the one she consulted with over designs and patterns. But they'd fall silent each time another inmate or guard passed them when they spoke.

They were clearly conspiring together. The question was about what.

One night, after work, when we were resting on our beds and I tried to soothe my throat with the brown liquid the SS called coffee, I asked Helene about her conversations with the lead seamstress.

"What do you mean? We're just talking about the new suit the commander's wife ordered for herself." She shrugged her shoulders, but I knew my sister too well. She was up to something, and the casualness of her answer told me that she was indeed hiding something from me.

"Come on, Helene. I know you."

"You should worry about getting over this cough, Sara," she said, her tone rather harsh.

"The Soviets are approaching Krakow. You heard it, too. They are so close, Helene. We won't have to wait much longer." I was encouraging her as much as I was myself. We just had to hang on a little longer. Hopefully. "Please don't do anything stupid now. Right before the end," I added.

Helene had never accepted that we'd abandoned our plan to escape.

"You don't know how long it will take the Soviets to get here. No one knows. It could be months. The Nazis won't give up so easily."

"What are you saying?"

"I'm saying that I want to fight. That I want to get out of here."

I stared at her. More in awe than in shock. Auschwitz hadn't broken her. And I admired her for it. "I don't want to lose you, Helene," I said as if to myself, but she had heard me.

"I need to do something, Sara. Please understand. I can't just sit there every day. Wait and sew. Sew for these people. These animals. I can't anymore."

"But what about me? We need to stay together!" If my sister managed to escape or was caught conspiring with the camp's underground—I couldn't finish the thought.

"Paul will look after you, and I'll find you later. I promise."

"You promised we'd stay together!" I jumped off the bed, knocking over the empty cup that had rested on it.

"Sara—" Helene had gotten up as well and put her hand on my shoulder, but I shook her off vehemently.

Stifling my cough, I marched off toward the washroom, my sister's betrayal stinging harder than the cough did my lungs.

———

Helene and I barely spoke after that. She tried to talk to me whenever we were alone, but I didn't let her. I usually ignored her attempts and walked off.

The end of the year was approaching, and with each passing day, Stalin's army drew nearer. I prayed they'd get to us before Helene could do whatever she planned to do.

In the early morning hours of the last day of the year, our SS guard, accompanied by two SS officers, entered our dormitories and shouted at us to get out of bed. We scrambled to our feet and stood at attention, shivering from the shock and cold.

The lead seamstress was called to their side. Without warning, one of the SS punched her in the stomach as soon as she stood in front of them. She crumpled to the floor, but our guard pulled her back up on her feet.

When they called Helene's number, I froze.

Out of the corner of my eye, I saw Helene straighten her shoulders and then proceed toward them as if she'd expected to be called up.

Helene too was greeted with a punch, though to her temple. She stumbled to the side but caught herself immediately. Both women were then dragged out, as our guard yelled at us to report to work immediately.

I stared at the door through which the SS had disappeared with my sister.

Helene.

My mind raced. Helene! What would happen to her now? Why had they come for her? They must have found out about whatever she'd been up to. Helene! Her name hammered in my mind like the punches of an SS guard. I could barely breathe.

The cough rose in my chest, and I fell into a terrible fit. Another seamstress tried to soothe me with her words and dragged me with her to the workshop.

I struggled through the day in a haze. We all felt lost without the lead seamstress there. No one wanted to take charge. We all wondered what the commander's wife thought about her lead seamstress being dragged off in the early morning hours. If she knew yet. For most of the day, we either finished what we had been working on individually or pretended to be busy. Our usual productivity and production had come to a halt. We were aimless and distraught.

Usually, the SS celebrated Sylvester, New Year's Eve, in a drunken state, shooting around wildly. Not this year. The camp was eerily still that night.

In hushed unison, inmates and SS lay with bated breath, awaiting the new year, which would hopefully bring the long-awaited liberation to the inmates or a desperate victory to the oppressors.

We, the seamstresses, barely noticed that the camp had gone quiet. For us, it was a night like every other night, with the exception that two of us were gone. Not knowing their fate was worse than the cold and hunger pains. Nevertheless, we clung to the hope that the two of them would still be alive the next morning.

I had to hope. Because it was all I had left.

CHAPTER 10
1945

The new year was only a few hours old when we were brutally awoken yet again. None of us had gotten any sleep that night. Our guard, together with other SS, ran us to the *Appelplatz* in the morning cold. My lungs stung and my cough erupted with a vengeance. I tried to suppress it without much success.

If this was selection, I would end up in the gas today, but in my weakened state and with my compromised lungs, I would at least succumb quickly.

When I finally caught my breath, I saw Helene standing off to the side between two SS officers. One of them grabbed her roughly by the arm and dragged her toward us. The lead seamstress was nowhere to be seen.

We were all lined up now. I feared the worst. For Helene. For myself. For all my fellow seamstresses. Maybe it was the day when we finally would meet death. After all our time in the camp.

I looked at Helene, trembling. My sister ...

My eyes fell on the gallows to the right. I understood now why we were there. It wasn't for selection. I would have to witness my sister being hung. My knees buckled, but I tried not to crumple to the ground. I looked at Helene. She stared blankly. I had to be strong for her. But how could I watch my sister die?

Helene stood in front of us, presented to us like a wounded animal or a condemned criminal. The SS officer screamed at her and pushed her toward the scaffold, but Helene stood her ground and didn't budge. Her lower jaw was pushed forward in defiance. The guard hit Helene in the back of her legs with his club and she dropped to the ground. Blood was crusted around her nostrils and there was a bluish-purple swelling near the bridge of her nose. They had already beaten her.

She suddenly looked wildly around in search of something or someone. Me? I searched for her eyes. When she finally found me in the crowd, a small smile crept into her face, and she gave me the subtlest of nods as if to reassure me. Or had I imagined it?

When a shot rang in the air, I jumped, and when I saw my sister's body fall to the side, I screamed. Hysterically. I had no control. I didn't care if they shot me, too. I wanted them to shoot me. But the SS officer just simply walked away while putting his handgun back in his holster.

I collapsed to the ground, but hands pulled me back up and steadied me. I tried to shake them off, but they wouldn't let go. My stomach twisted and I vomited right there.

That night, back in my bed with my sister's empty beside mine, I hoped, begged, and prayed for death.

My condition deteriorated rapidly after that. The cough rocked my body continuously. I didn't complain or resist when I was told that I would be transferred to the sick block again. I had given up, just like Alice had. And once you had given up, no one could save you.

Helene was gone. I was alone now. My family was dead. Father, Mother, Aunt Irene, little Ruth, and both my elder sisters.

In the sick block, I was told I had pneumonia. I developed a fever again and drifted in and out of consciousness. I was neither dead nor alive.

The kind Jewish nurse kept me alive as much as she could, but she also knew I had become a Muselmann. I no longer cared to eat. I no longer cared to live.

Despite my own neglect and due to the nurse not giving up on me, my fever eventually broke, and I got better. The cough lingered on, but my health improved.

When the SS doctor came to my bedside, I was sitting up and eating.

The woman in the bed next to me was selected for the gas. She was skin and bones. Her shallow, ragged breathing was the only indication that she was still alive.

To my own astonishment, I no longer feared selection.

———

Days later, in the early morning hours, when it was still completely dark outside, a tumult arose outside the windows of the infirmary and woke me up. The chaos soon made its way into the sick block. Prisoners came rushing in looking for their friends or family, saying that the camp was being evacuated to the Reich's interior. The SS was packing up themselves, they said, raiding *Kanada* and taking with them what they could.

We wondered what would happen to us, the sick and infirm.

An hour later, an SS officer appeared and yelled that all able-bodied prisoners in the sick block were to report to evacuate the camp as well. Most of us were too sick to comply and leave our beds. But what would happen to us if we couldn't evacuate with the rest?

Only moments after the SS had left, Paul came in. He had come! I hadn't seen him in a long time. For a moment, I wondered if he knew about Helene. He must have heard. He stood at the foot of my bed, his head and clothing covered in a thin layer of snow, his face frozen.

My heart beat faster, and I sat up in my bed. He smiled at me and moved to the side of my bed to be closer to me. I looked around to see if any of the medical staff had noticed him, but they were busy packing up what they could because they were leaving as well.

No one cared anymore.

Paul dusted off the snow and sat beside me. He blew into his hands and took one of mine. His were ice cold. "How are you? One of the seamstresses told me you were back in here." The concern in his voice and face gave me immediate comfort, and I squeezed his hand in gratitude. "Are you able to get up and leave with everyone else? Can you believe we're finally getting out of here?"

I lowered my eyes and swallowed hard.

Paul squeezed my hand. "I'm so sorry, Sara. I heard. I tried to write to you, but I could no longer get any messages to you. It was impossible." Tears welled, and I swallowed again. We sat in silence for a few minutes.

"Why is Helene gone, Paul?" I looked him straight in the eyes, but it was he who lowered his gaze.

"She wanted to leave, Sara. No one could talk her out of it," he said quietly.

"But how?"

"She was sewing herself an SS women's guard uniform. She wanted to disguise herself and just walk out of here."

"But when? When would she have had time and a place to do that?" But as soon as I had finished my question, I knew. We were mending the guards' uniforms occasionally. She could have easily sewn one in plain sight.

Paul shifted uneasily and looked around. "We need to get you up, Sara. You need to leave with the rest of us."

I stared at him. "I can't. There's no way I can't get up and march."

"You have to. You don't have a choice." I closed my eyes. He didn't understand how weak I still was. Typhus and pneumonia had taken their toll on my body. I looked like a corpse. But Paul wasn't giving up so easily. "They're marching us into Germany, Sara. Don't you want to go back? Get out of here?" He was relentless.

"Of course, I do. But I can't. I'm too weak."

"They'll shoot everyone left behind." My heart stopped at the urgency in his voice. It made him sound shrill. I squeezed my eyes shut. "You need to get up. You need to leave with the other female prisoners. You must. Everyone is leaving, even the sick. Look around. They're destroying all the evidence." He paused for a moment, but I refused to open my eyes. "You're the evidence, Sara," Paul added, his tone suddenly cold.

I shuddered at Paul's cruel words, but I knew he wasn't trying to hurt me, that he wanted to save my life.

I opened my eyes but avoided looking at him. I craned my neck to look around the sick ward. Only a third of the patients seemed to be leaving. The rest of us were just too sick or weak to do the same. My own body was done. How could I go on this long march back to Germany in the dead of winter? That was impossible. I was dead either way.

And I couldn't go on. Not without Helene.

"She would have wanted you to go, you know, to be strong," Paul said, sounding a little bitter. His words stung, and I turned my head away from him toward the window. I knew he had risked his life to come see me under the cover of the evacuation chaos. He had come. For me. But I couldn't go. That was the brutal, bitter truth.

I had made it this far, but I couldn't go on anymore.

Paul's eyes locked on the door. He hastily pulled out a piece of paper and a stump of a pencil. He hurriedly scribbled something down and pressed the paper into my hand. I didn't look at it.

"This is my uncle's address in Haifa. Please, Sara, come to Haifa." He paused. I still didn't look at him but stared at the window, the dirt of which prevented me from getting a clear view of the chaos outside. "I love you, Sara," he murmured. A tear ran down my face. He put his hand on my cheek. "Please, hide. Anywhere. Don't let them shoot you. The Soviets are almost here. If you make it out of here alive, come to Haifa. Please. I want to be with you." His voice was hoarse, and I turned my head toward him. Tears were swimming in his eyes.

I swallowed and nodded. "I promise."

Palestine. Helene was meant to go to Palestine. Not me.

I swallowed again and closed my eyes.

Paul kissed my forehead, then I felt his weight lift off my bedside and he was gone. Maybe forever.

If I survived, how would I make it to Palestine by myself? It was impossible.

I looked at the paper in the palm of my hand but closed my fist around it. I closed my eyes again, unwilling to watch the tumult around me.

Throughout the day, fewer and fewer doctors and nurses appeared. The camp grew quieter and quieter with each passing hour. The kind Jewish nurse who'd nursed me back to health both times also took her leave. She wasn't allowed to stay, she said but was forced to march to Germany with the rest of the camp prisoners.

After she had left, it grew silent in the sick block.

By evening, rumors swirled among us, who had been left behind, that most columns of prisoners had been marched out of the camp. What would happen to the rest of us now? Should I hide as Paul had told me? Most of us were not able to move.

I decided to leave it to fate, too weak to get up.

The eerie stillness and silence of the camp was only interrupted by the unrelenting fighting we heard in the distance. We expected to be picked up for the gas or get the injection that would take us out of our misery at any moment. But no one came for us. We waited for liberation or death. But dying wasn't as easily done as one thought.

I fantasized about it. I thought about getting up and stepping out of the infirmary. Maybe a guard on the tower would take me out. Or I could walk out somehow and touch the high-voltage fence. Something. But I couldn't move. So I waited and coughed and waited more. Death had to come eventually.

Death did come for some in the infirmary. Without doctors and nurses, and worst of all, no food, several of the sick succumbed. The stench of death and rot had replaced the smell of bleach that had hung in the air before. The SS had harassed the nurses to keep the floors clean. With each passing day, I missed the familiar scent of bleach more and more.

We usually found the corpses in the morning hours in their beds. Or they had fallen to the ground beside their beds during the night, staring wide-eyed into nothing, their faces a grotesque grimace as if death was as painful as our existence. We were too weak to remove them. They kept lying where they'd taken their last breath.

Those of us still alive in the infirmary were left completely unguarded. All the staff had left. So had all the SS and guards. There was no heating, no food. The rats came out every night, feeding on the corpses. We were left to starve, left to die.

Outside the windows of the infirmary, we saw columns of smoke lingering. One of us, able to walk somewhat, was sent to inquire. She came back shortly and reported that the SS had destroyed the crematoria and that the smoke of burnt human flesh no longer rose from there anymore, but that the SS had left burning heaps of documents and that the air was filled with a cleansing kind of smoke and littered with a million tiny pieces of paper which we, inside, had mistaken for falling snow.

Right when she had finished her report, an SS guard stumbled in. So not all SS had left yet. We froze, the fear making us hold our collective breaths. But he ignored us completely, the dead and the living. He made his way to the office. Only a few minutes later, he appeared with an armful of papers. Medical records? He rushed outside only to come back moments later with another guard to retrieve more documents. They did so many times.

We lay still on our beds that day as if dead, and as such they treated us.

When it had been hours since their last return, those of us who could, started moving around. I sat up in my bed. It was unbearably cold, and the block hadn't been heated in days. Neither had we eaten in just as long. I stole the blanket from the corpse in the neighboring bed and added it to the ones that already tried to keep me warm.

Tomorrow, I would try to venture out to see if I could find anything edible. It was time to get up. The hunger pains of the last few days had been worse than when I'd recovered from typhus.

The next morning, I sat up and swung my legs to the side of the bed. Immediately, blackness flooded my head. I felt faint and squeezed my eyes shut, breathing heavily. When the dizziness subsided, I opened my eyes and slowly pushed myself up and out of bed. I had to steady myself but felt exhilarated to finally be up and stand on my own two feet again.

A French woman with bulging and filthy bandages adorning her head volunteered to venture out of the building with me.

The camp lay completely still in the bright morning sun against which we had to shield our eyes. We ignored the corpses that littered the grounds all around and headed for the kitchen. A murder of crows was picking at some of the bodies. When we stumbled past them, they flew up, cawing angrily and loudly.

My feet quickly grew numb on the frozen ground. I was winded. I had to stop several times, my exhausted and starved body needing a break. After what seemed like hours, we arrived at the kitchen which appeared deserted in the morning sun. Inside, however, we found two male prisoners who were also foraging for food. They'd found a big sack of potatoes. With big, hollow eyes, they looked at us grimly.

I asked them if they would share their spoils with the sick in the infirmary. To our great relief, they agreed. We were human again.

Getting to the kitchen had been the easy part. Carrying the potatoes back to the sick block posed another challenge entirely. We found an old bucket and together, the French woman, who had introduced herself as Marie, and I carried the bucket of potatoes back to the infirmary, having to stop frequently.

When we couldn't go on, we sat down to take a break. Marie asked me about myself, but I didn't feel like thinking or speaking about the past and sharing my story with this stranger, so she told me hers. How she'd fought for the French resistance and how one of her fellow resistance fighters had given the Gestapo her name and hiding place and that of others under the duress of torture. She said she didn't blame him, knowing that the horrible means of torture the Gestapo used made even the strongest sing.

After Marie had shared her story, I began to share mine. Like the gushing water of a broken dam, the words flooded out of me. I told her about my parents and siblings, my home, Salzhausen, sewing, Ravensbrück, the fashion salon, Alice, her baby, Helene, and Paul. I told her everything. I shared it all. Afterward, I felt better than I had in ages.

Marie and I smiled at each other.

The sun no longer stood high in the sky. Stiff from having sat in the cold for so long, we got up and continued our journey with our precious cargo.

Back in the sick block, we used bedding to light a fire and the wooden remains of a chair to cook the potatoes. The warmth of the fire and the taste of food lifted my spirits and those of us remaining in the sick block instantaneously. Marie and I shared in taking care of and feeding those in the infirmary too sick to do so themselves. We were the nurses now.

The next day, after the sun had set, I ventured out again. Alone this time. Marie was looking after the sick while I sought more supplies. I knew where to find what I was looking for. I'd go to the building of my former work. It was dangerous, but my trip to the kitchen had emboldened me and we desperately needed supplies to take care of the ill.

I knew if there were any SS left in the camp, they would probably be at headquarters. But to my great relief, the building appeared deserted when I approached it. Papers were strewn about in front of it, and former fires built to burn documents were still glimmering.

Carefully and slowly, I made my way up the stairs. I thought of Paul. How we had met on these very steps. I smiled to myself. The thought of Paul accompanied me all the way to the hallway in the basement where he and I had kissed. It seemed like a dream now, and I wondered if it had actually happened.

When I reached the door to the former fashion salon, my thoughts turned to Helene. I was unprepared for the sudden onslaught of grief. I pressed my forehead against the door and sobbed uncontrollably. I didn't know how long I remained in that state, but eventually, my tears ran out, and I pushed open the door to the salon.

Inside, fabrics, cut-out patterns, and other sewing materials were strewn around as if left in a hurry. I walked in slowly. When I came up next to one of the sewing machines, I ran my hand across the cold metal and lettering. I stared at it for a moment, wondering if I would ever be able to sew again. With a sigh, I started to collect fabric and half-finished dresses. I took as much as I could carry. We desperately needed bandaging, clothing, and fuel.

The commander's wife would not be happy if she knew what I did with her orders and materials.

Before I left the workshop, I spotted a fur coat in the very back of the room next to the little changing cabin we'd set up for our clients. I wondered who had left it. I grabbed it and threw it on immediately.

When I walked past the mirror in the little changing room, the corner of my eye captured a ghastly vision. Hesitantly, I walked back to take a look at myself in the mirror from which the wives of the SS had smiled at themselves. The image that stared back at me, however, was dreadful.

My hair was one big matted knot and large junks were missing across my head. My face was drained of all color, and my eyes were sunken deep into my head, large dark shadows encircling them. The sore on my lip was a large blister that was oozing with a yellowish liquid. My collar bones were sticking out, threatening to pierce my thin paper-like yellow skin. I was a corpse. The brown fur coat was lush and shiny, standing in stark contrast to the body that was wearing it.

Swallowing hard, I tore my stare away from the mirror, wondering for a moment if I would ever look like my old self again.

I left the fashion salon with both arms full of supplies. I thought about heading down to our former dormitories but decided against it. It would be too painful to see Helene's bed.

A week later, we heard the fanfares of the Red Army enter the camp. Hours later, Soviet soldiers came into the sick block. They immediately covered their mouths and noses. With muffled voices and broken German, they told us we were liberated. They said it so matter-of-factly and as if it was the most ordinary thing in the world to say to someone, that we just stared at them blankly. I had always envisioned this moment as something grand and exciting. Something that would make us shout for joy, jump up and down, dance, and sing. Cry, even. That moment wasn't any of that.

In the days that followed our liberation, Polish and Soviet health personnel took over our sick block and Marie and my duties. We were cared for again. Clean sheets, civilian winter clothing, hot soups and bread, medicine, and warm blankets—found in *Kanada* I was told, saved our lives once more.

With each passing day, I felt less fatigued, and my strength returned. The first few nights after our liberators had taken over, the death count among us was still high. But eventually, fewer and fewer former prisoners succumbed, until one day, no deaths were reported. Everyone around me started to look human again, so I assumed the same was happening to me. I was desperately hoping it was, though I didn't dare look in a mirror again, even when one was offered to me.

When former fellow sick prisoners, somewhat recovered, started leaving, I knew I would leave soon too, and I needed to make a decision. I had written to Georg shortly after liberation. Not only to tell him that I was still alive while his family was gone but also to inquire if there was a chance he would welcome me and give me a home. Two weeks later, a member of a Jewish help organization appeared to tell me that they were taking me and some of the others to America. In two days' time, I'd be on a truck to a train, which would take me to a ship heading for New York.

Two days, and I would finally leave the camp.

After the man had left, I pulled out Paul's note. I had to make peace with the fact that I wouldn't keep my promise to him. Georg was my family, and he waited for me to join him.

I missed Paul terribly, and I hoped he had been liberated too and had made his way to his uncle in Palestine. With time, Paul would forget about me, and with time, I would too.

I held the note in my fist for the rest of that day, fearing the moisture of my palm would erase the penciled handwriting.

When I went to bed that night, sleep escaped me. Rolling over in my bed and clasping Paul's note tightly, I let the tears come. Grieving him would help me move on.

Two days later, the man returned with other workers from his help organization and told us to gather up our belongings. I had none, so I stood in front of the infirmary, shielding my eyes from the pale winter sun and waiting with the others to leave.

A hand rested on my shoulder, and I turned around. I looked into Marie's smiling face, her head no longer wrapped in bandages. She pulled me into a big hug. I couldn't remember the last time I had experienced that simple pleasure. Maybe it had been Mother's, maybe Alice's. I wasn't sure. I swallowed hard. The warmth of the embrace tightened my throat, and I tried to stifle the sob that worked its way up.

I let Maria hold me. I would let her hug me for as long as she wanted.

She whispered, "Go find him!" I wanted to stay in our embrace, but I let go of her. My puzzled look encouraged her to explain. "Your friend. What was his name? Paul?" I lowered my head and quietly shook my head. "I'm going to America. My brother got me a visa."

"Oh, I see. I just thought that ..." She trailed off. After a moment's pause, she added, "Well, I wish you all the luck in the world, Sara. Live bravely, will you?"

As she walked away, I followed her with my eyes until I realized that those around me had begun moving. A big Red Cross truck off to the side was already loading people.

I'd be leaving Auschwitz today. At last.

How surreal to finally leave the camp. After everything. I looked around one last time to take it all in. For the rest of my life, I would try my hardest to forget every single detail about that place. I didn't want to remember anything about it. Ever. And that was a promise I intended to keep until my dying breath.

With a resolve I hadn't felt in months, I let a man help me climb up onto the truck. When the vehicle jerked forward and the cold late winter air blew into my face and hair, it felt like I was being cleansed in a way that water hadn't been able to.

As we rumbled down the road, I said my goodbyes to all I had lost.

The cold wind made my eyes water. My vision of the camp started to blur, the buildings swimming away.

When we reached the Krakow train station, we were told our train would leave in the evening and that we would have time to take a walk or rest until then. I chose to venture out and explore the city. I asked if anyone wanted to join me, but the others declined. I didn't mind, though, and set out on my own.

I'd never been to Krakow. I was amazed that war had not marked the city. It had remained largely unscathed, its beautiful architecture preserved. The bustling streets stood in stark contrast to where I'd been, and I felt like covering my ears from the noises surrounding me.

After I'd walked down a few streets and turned a few corners, I found myself at the farmer's market. People were shopping, talking, laughing. It was as if there never had been a war. Maybe it had all just been a very bad dream. But it hadn't been. The price I'd paid had been too steep for it to have been a dream.

No one could dream up the horrors of the last few years.

I spotted a bench and sat down. The dying winter sun was warming my face. I breathed in deeply. Spring would be coming soon. And I would be in New York then. With Georg. And Clara, he had told me in one of his letters. We had each other. Three of us had survived.

I looked at the people walking between stands and vendors, their arms and baskets full of all kinds of foods. I marveled at the abundance of it all.

My stomach rumbled, and I got up. It was time to return to the train station, but there was one problem. I had no idea which way to go. I was completely lost.

I would need to ask for directions, but I only spoke a few words of Polish I'd picked up during my summers with Bobe and Zayde in Chelm and from Mother, and none of them included the word for train station.

A woman was coming toward me. She looked friendly enough, so I lifted my hand and apologized to her in Polish. She stopped but looked me up and down, her brows furrowed. I asked her in German for the train station. She stumbled several feet back and screeched

"German!" in Polish, pointing at me, her eyes wild. People around us stopped what they were doing and stared at me, many with angry faces and balled fists. I raised both of my hands in defense and yelled "Jew" in Polish, hitting my chest with my hands, but people started cussing around me and spitting on the ground. Someone pushed me from behind.

I stumbled away from the crowd that had gathered and broke out into a run. The cold air stung my lungs, but I didn't care. I ran and ran, amazed at the strength I had.

It took me two hours to find the train station. When I entered, the beautiful large clock told me I'd made it in time with a few minutes to spare. I wiped my forehead with my sleeve, and my eyes fell on the schedule of trains leaving Krakow which was posted across from me.

For a minute my eyes rested on it. I looked back up at the clock. It was time to go to the platform. When I arrived, some from my group had already begun to board one of the passenger cars. I walked over to the nice man who was bringing us to America. He looked relieved when he saw me.

"I won't be coming with you," I said to him. He stared at me. "I need to go home."

"How will you get there?" He asked in perfect German, his face friendly.

"I was hoping I could ask you for some money to buy another train ticket."

He laughed but nodded. He reached into the inner pocket of his winter coat and pulled out a small bundle of money. "Here. Take it."

I grabbed it from him, gave him a grateful smile, and started running again.

I could make the other train if I hurried.

———

My heart pounded when the train pulled into Salzhausen in the evening. It seemed years ago since I'd left my hometown where I had been born and lived most of my childhood until the Nazis had cut it short.

There was no need to return to my former home. It had burned down. There was only one reason I'd stopped in Salzhausen before going on to Altstädt. I wanted to go to the cemetery.

On the way there, I kept my eyes low to the ground, wanting to avoid recognizing anyone. I didn't want to look into the eyes of those who had just stood by.

The cemetery lay cold and barren in the dying light. I made my way through the rows of gravestones and found the one I was looking for. I placed my hand over the lettering and swallowed hard. At least Father had a place of rest. I took a pebble from the ground and placed it carefully on top of the gravestone while saying the Kaddish my Mother had taught me.

Mother didn't have a grave. Neither did Aunt Irene, little Ruth, Alice, and Helene.

I left the cemetery with a heavy heart.

A light drizzle accompanied me on my way through the fields to Altstädt. It was dark. Aunt Irene's house was my next stop, but I wasn't sure what to do after that. Would I stay there? Could I stay there? Could I live all alone in Altstädt? In her house? In a town where some of its citizens had ostracized and persecuted us? What if they still hated me because I was a Jew? And could I look into the eyes of those who had murdered my family? What if I came across them?

With each thought, my steps toward Altstädt slowed. I became hesitant and regretted my decision to not go to America.

When the dark outlines of the houses of Altstädt were finally in front of me, I thought of Alice, Hershel, and Ruth whom I had so often visited. Hershel. I'd never heard what had become of him. Before going to Aunt Irene's house, I would stop by their flat to see if I could find out anything. And if there was nothing, I would make my way to the house of Hershel's parents.

With a plan set and a new resolve, I fell into a quicker pace again.

I rang the bell of Alice's and Hershel's former apartment, but no one opened. I looked up at the building. No light came from the windows of their former flat. I walked on to his parents' house next but it, too, seemed unoccupied and abandoned.

Stepping away from the house and walking down the street I had so often done, I felt abandoned. I was utterly alone. I shuddered and noticed how hungry and tired I was. Aunt Irene's house would be a welcome refuge. I knew where she had hidden a key in the back. But I was afraid of how I would feel alone in a house once occupied by my family who were all gone now.

I would rest and decide what to do tomorrow. I yearned for the bed I'd shared with Clara there.

To my surprise, light shone from the windows of Aunt Irene's house. I went around the back and found the same potted plant sitting on the windowsill next to the back door. If the pot was still there, the key would be, too. I lifted the pot, but no key was underneath. After setting the pottery back down, I lifted it up again. Maybe I had missed it? It still wasn't there.

I decided to make my way to the front door and just ring the bell. Someone was in there. I had no idea who, but I would find out. There were voices inside, but no one came to the door. People were reluctant to answer their doors after dark, especially when they didn't expect anyone. But this was different. It was my aunt's house. I rang the bell again, unwilling to give up. I was exhausted and tired.

Maybe Hershel was living here now. Or his parents. Or some other family member.

I rang the bell again. Twice. And added a couple of knocks on the door. Irregular heavy steps approached the front door and I held my breath. The door opened, and the face of a man appeared. I fell back a step. I didn't know him. I had never seen him before. A stranger. He was missing a leg and stared at me impatiently.

"My aunt used to live here," I blurted out in confusion. Who was this man?

His expression changed from impatience to a mixture of disdain and guilt. "We live here now," he said gruffly. A woman and a child appeared behind him, their eyes wide. The woman looked apologetic but cowered at the man's scowl. I tried to get a glimpse of the inside, but the man shuffled to the side when he saw me peek past him. "This is our home now," he added and shut the door in my face.

I stumbled farther back and down the stairs. At first, I walked swiftly, then I broke into a run. I ran all the way back to Salzhausen, through the dark fields, over roots and rocks until I reached the train station. I didn't know how I was able to run that far in my state, but I did. My lungs stung and my sides hurt, but I ignored my body's protests. I had to get away.

There was nothing there for me anymore. No family, no home.

The train station lay deserted in the dark. There would be no train until the morning. I went to the platform and spotted a bench to curl up on. It felt damp, but I didn't mind.

Shivering in the cold, I scolded myself for abandoning my journey to America.

A hand rested on my shoulder, and I looked up into the face of a kind old woman. "Are you lost, dear?"

I shook my head in confusion and pushed myself up. I grimaced at the pain in my shoulder and back from sleeping on the hard wooden bench all night. "The first train won't leave for another hour, child," the woman said. She wore a headscarf and a basket dangled on her arm. It was full of dandelions she seemed to have picked.

"I don't have any money for the train," I blurted out, fully realizing my predicament in the clear morning air. I breathed in deeply. My lungs still stung. They'd never be the same.

"I have a bike if you would like to have it. It used to belong to my son," she offered and eyed me carefully. "Would you like a cup of tea? I live over there." She pointed at a small house that stood alone under a group of linden trees.

I remembered that house. I'd passed it many times as a child. I looked at the woman more closely. She was familiar. Perhaps I'd seen her in the streets of Salzhausen or in one of the shops.

"I'd like a cup of tea," I said and followed her to her house. If I couldn't get on a train, I would need a bike.

The house lay still and looked deserted. She seemed to live alone. I followed her into her kitchen. She put the kettle on and motioned for me to sit down. I looked around. On the wall were several family pictures. One of them was of her son. He was wearing an SS uniform. A black ribbon adorned the frame.

I shifted uncomfortably in my seat, staring at the old woman's back as she poured her brew into cups. I looked from her to the door. I could just escape. Run from her. But I stayed rooted in my seat, the SS man smiling faintly at me. I shuddered.

Just as I was getting up, the old woman turned around, carrying two teacups that shook slightly on their plate. She placed them on the table with her trembling hands and sat down across from me. "I hope you like dandelion tea."

I nodded uncomfortably and mumbled a "yes." I had never had dandelion tea before. I put the cup to my lips. The bitter warmth reminded me of the bitterness of the brown liquid we had been forced to drink in Auschwitz. I put the cup down.

"I knew your father, child," the old woman said. "And your grandfather. They made my late husband's suits. Wonderful suits," she said, looking up at the family pictures on the wall.

"So, you know me, remember me?" I asked. I was surprised that the woman knew my family well and had recognized me.

"Yes, I remember your whole family. Your mother, a very kind woman. You children." She eyed me carefully again. "I'd heard what happened to your father and home. Shameful!" She looked into her cup, her face unreadable. After a moment, she peered into my eyes, her voice a mere whisper. "What happened to your family? Your mother? Sisters?"

I stared at her blankly. Did she really not know? What had happened to all of us? To the Jews? "I need to go now," I said abruptly and got up. She looked hurt, but I ignored her. "Could I use that bike?" I asked.

"Yes, you may." I followed her outside the back of her house. An old shed stood in the far corner. "Do you know where you will go?" She asked. I shook my head. "There's a lot of refugees now. I heard they house them in camps," she added.

I froze. Camps?

She looked at me with raised eyebrows. "With so many people not knowing where to go, the Americans have set up temporary camps, people are saying. Maybe you will find your family there." I swallowed hard at her last words.

She opened the shed. The bike looked old and rusty. It was covered in spider webs and debris. I brushed some of it away with my hand. Out of the corner of my eye, I saw a pump to the side and under her watchful eye, I filled the tires with air, hoping it would hold.

"You can take the pump with you. Let me wrap you up some bread for your journey, too." I wanted to protest but knew better. It would need it.

———

I was on the road for three months. Kind farmers and their wives let me work for food and shelter on my way. Working in fields and orchards and sleeping in barns. But I never stayed longer than a few days. I got restless quickly and was eager to move on. Where to and to what purpose, I didn't know. I was aimless. But to my own surprise, I didn't mind. I only felt drawn to go south, unsure why.

Sometimes there were already others in the barns where I was sheltered. It seemed as if all of Europe was on the move. Former forced laborers and camp prisoners trying to return home but also prisoners of war and German refugees making their way west after having been forced out of homes in the former Eastern parts of the Reich. I was wary of them and kept to myself. But I overheard their conversations.

One night, with straw poking my back and an old smelly blanket trying to keep me warm, I found a purpose and destination for my aimless journey. A woman and five men, Hungarian and Austrian Jews, who had also been in Auschwitz, spoke of different kinds of camps, similar to the ones the old woman had mentioned. They called them Displaced Persons Camps. There would be food and shelter, schooling, and vocational training, they reported. The woman and the men were also trying to find their relatives and these camps would be a good starting point to either find them or any information about where to look next.

The authorities and help organizations were registering incoming persons. They also spoke of going to Palestine. It made me think of Paul. Maybe I could find him at one of those camps. And I could inquire about Hershel.

That night I wasn't able to find any sleep.

In the morning, I asked if I could join them. They agreed, the woman being particularly glad that she was no longer the only female. In return for adopting me as their new traveling companion, I let them take turns riding the bike. They didn't need to know that it was the bike of a former SS officer.

Along the way, they sang Zionist songs, making me miss Helene terribly, but I fell in step with them, feeling oddly comforted by the zealousness of the lyrics.

We arrived at a camp two weeks later. It was already overcrowded, but the Americans who ran the camp accepted everyone in our group, except the Austrian Jews and me. They turned us away because we were German. The Austrians protested but to no avail. The camp only housed foreigners and no German nationalities were accepted. But they told us about another camp and gave us directions. They said that it was located outside of Munich near the Starnberger Lake.

I'd heard Oma Ruth talk about that lake. She'd spent her family's summer vacations there as a child.

The camp lay on the outskirts of a town near the Bavarian capital. I had avoided big cities on my journey and was glad we were able to bypass Munich. When we arrived, we were asked if we suffered from tuberculosis since the camp was also a TB sanatorium. We all denied we did and underwent a thorough medical exam. I hoped my weak lungs would mean I could get some treatments for them there. Pneumonia had scarred them. Unfortunately, I was denied treatment because their sick ward was overcrowded already. Nevertheless, I was glad that the Americans had accepted me at the camp. They gave me new papers, and I was housed in a block with former women prisoners from Dachau. I kept to myself again. I didn't want to hear their stories. We all had one.

A few days after my arrival, I had to report to have my schooling evaluated. They also asked me about my profession. I told them I had none. I was told which vocational training programs the camp offered. I shuddered when they asked me if I wanted to become a seamstress.

I told them that I wanted to become a teacher, and I was assigned as an assistant teacher to one of the classrooms of the camp's school. The children in the class, who should have been reading and writing and doing simple math at their age, were illiterate and never had any formal instruction. Hitler had deprived them of an education, but I would now help rectify that.

I felt at home in the classroom and close to Aunt Irene and Helene.

Every day after school, I went to the clerk's office to inquire about Paul and Hershel, but there never was any information on either of them. If they had registered at one of the DP camps, the Americans would have known. I was told that not everyone came to an American DP camp, though, but that many survivors were also leaving Europe and some of them had returned to their homelands.

Paul had wanted to go to Palestine as soon as he was liberated. And I had promised to meet him there. I couldn't picture Paul waiting around in a DP camp. But I had also heard that the British government was restricting immigration to Palestine due to Arab pressures. Knowing Paul, I was sure that he had found his way there. Somehow. The question was if I should do the same.

I wrote to Georg and Clara. The only sister I had left now had already made the journey to America. In his letters, my brother chastised me for having stayed and urged me to leave as soon as possible. In one of his correspondences, he also notified me that Hershel had died in prison, days after his arrest. The knowledge of his death hit me harder than I expected. It brought the pain of the deaths of little Ruth, Alice, and their baby back to me.

A whole young family gone.

I missed them and wondered if the pain over their deaths would ever cease or if it would stay with me for the rest of my life.

After a few weeks in the DP camp, I fell ill yet again and was admitted to the sanatorium to recover from another bout of pneumonia. I wondered if that would be my existence going forward. A sickly shell of a person with no family whose lungs would eventually give out. However, after four weeks in the sanatorium, I was better and I was released to get back to my teaching duties.

I settled in and started to consider the camp my home. It indeed felt like a village. We had the school, a newspaper, sports games, a hospital, and vocational training programs. People got married and began to have babies. There was laughter and celebration but also many moments of silence.

Different help organizations tried to locate loved ones and arrange for the camp residents to emigrate or return to their homelands. However, with the rise of communist regimes in Eastern Europe and the prevailing antisemitism, the former homelands of the Jews of Europe ceased to become a viable option. And there were many like me whose homes were now occupied by others and who no longer felt at home in their former towns and villages where they had been ostracized and persecuted. And most, like me, had no or very little family left where they were from.

The DP camp became my home, but I knew I needed to fight my complacency and not get too settled. I needed to make a decision where I wanted to go. I had to set myself a deadline. Georg continued to urge me to come to America in his letters. Clara did the same. Eventually, I gave in and applied for another visa, but what about Paul? I had promised him. But going to Palestine? So far away? All by myself? It seemed as daunting as ever. More daunting than to get to a port and onto a ship for a long journey to America. I knew someone would greet me upon arrival. But I had no assurance that I would find and meet Paul in Palestine.

In the meantime, teaching became my solace. The teacher I assisted in the classroom told me she would leave for Palestine in the new year. Her name was Nellie and she also had lost her family.

Nellie was five years my senior and originally from Berlin. She reminded me so much of Helene. Her hair and her personality. Her wit and her defiance. I often sought to be close to her. She made me laugh and I caught myself mistaking her for my late sister. It scared me, but I knew her presence was healing for me. We became friends. Her young students loved her while merely tolerating me.

After a few weeks, she asked me if I wanted to join her on her journey to Palestine. I surprised myself when I said yes. Several others wanted to join, too. We had a small group that would leave in the new year. I anticipated our day of departure with both excitement and dread, but I wanted to stay with Nellie, and the prospect of keeping my promise to Paul uplifted me.

I wrote to Georg and Clara and told them about my decision, but I left out the true reasons why I would go to Palestine. I knew they would already be displeased with me as is, let alone if I told them I'd follow a man to a place where I had no family. I didn't look forward to their next letter, but I felt resolute about my decision. I would leave Germany and Europe behind and go to Palestine where Mother and Aunt Irene had wanted to send Helene and me, and where my sister had always wished to go. It was ironic that it would be me who would now end up there. I no longer felt reluctant to leave. I was keeping my promise to Paul, and in a way, I felt like I was honoring Helene.

With Nellie as a travel companion and friend, I knew I could make the long and uncertain journey. I would find Paul, and we would begin a new life in a new land where our people lived.

Once I'd made my decision, I thought of Paul every day and dreamed of him at night. The hope of seeing him again and being with him gave me the kind of motivation I hadn't felt in a very long time, and it gave me courage—the courage to leave and the courage to begin a new life in a strange land.

CHAPTER 11

1946

Nellie and the rest of us left the DP camp in February. We didn't tell them where we were heading. We had no visas to enter Palestine legally.

We took a train to Venice. The beautiful train ride through the Alps stood in stark contrast to the fateful train journey in cattle cars to Auschwitz that my family and I had been forced on. Our group spent the ten-hour train ride mostly in silence, wistfully staring at the towering snow-covered mountains that flew by. We almost felt like tourists, but we weren't. We were refugees who had experienced so much loss to which we now added the loss of our homelands. Everything familiar would be forever left in the past, together with the loved ones we had lost. We were rootless, homeless, and stateless.

Leaving for Palestine made sense, but it made us all pensive.

When we arrived in Venice, throngs of people lined the waterways of the city and hundreds of gondolas dotted the canals. It was Carnival, and I'd never seen anything like it. The beautifully crafted gondolas, the happy young men steering them. Some people were even dancing on them. Smiling, waving, happy people everywhere.

It was as if the war had never happened. As if the people of Venice had never seen its horrors. Maybe most of them hadn't. I didn't know, but all the celebrating, all the colors seemed jarring after everything I had seen and lost. Yet, I let the mayhem pull me along, and after a little while, I found myself smiling.

For a few moments that day, I forgot about all that had happened to me, my family, my people.

The next morning, when Venice still lay sleeping like two lovers, and the many gondolas were bopping empty and quietly tied up along the sides of the canals, we left the city to travel on to the nearby Island of Pellestrina, which separated the Venetian Lagoon from the Adriatic Sea. Nellie had found passage for us on a ship that was leaving for Palestine in March. She told us that there were organizations that helped Jews reach the Holy Land, even if it had to be illegal. She had met with them several times while at the DP camp and had secured train tickets and ship passage for herself, me, and the rest of our small group.

All we had to do now was wait.

———————

After four weeks of waiting, sitting around with nothing to do but read and walk the island aimlessly, the day of our departure finally arrived. My anxiety had increased with each approaching day, but Nellie tried to reassure me as best as she could.

The morning, when we were finally set to sail, I was as calm as the lake in Chelm where my sisters and I had spent many summers swimming. But when I stood on the boardwalk, looking up at the schooner in front of me, my anxiety returned.

I'd never been on a ship before. It wasn't particularly grand and the thought of spending days on this boat made me very uneasy. Helene wouldn't have minded and considered it an adventure. She would have scolded me for my reluctance, complaints, and anxiety.

I swallowed, gripped the small suitcase in my hand harder, and made my way on board.

Most of the 250 passengers were displaced persons, many of them survivors like us, who were seeking a new life, a new beginning in Palestine. But we lacked one thing: an official entry permit. For that reason, we were to rendezvous along the way with another ship which would then continue with us to Palestine, landing in the middle of the night on the shores of Tel Aviv. It sounded dangerous and risky to me, but we had no other way to get to Palestine.

I was glad I wasn't alone. Nellie was with me, and my promise to Paul made me determined. I assumed that Paul probably wouldn't have had any trouble getting permission to enter British-mandate Palestine because he had family in Haifa. But even if he hadn't secured a visa, I was sure Paul would have gotten there somehow, one way or another.

Unlike him, Nellie, I, and the rest of our group only had the option of illegal immigration like most people on the ship. The British government had agreed with Arab demands to limit Jewish immigration and established a blockade in the Mediterranean. Fortunately for us, enough networks were willing to help find a way around the blockade and bring the surviving Jews of Europe to Palestine.

On our first day, the sea was smooth, and I enjoyed the stiff breeze on my face and breathing in the salty air. The sea looked beautiful, and I felt relaxed. On the third day, we were given two sets of bad news. For one, we wouldn't meet the other ship that was supposed to take us to Tel Aviv. In addition, we were warned by the captain that starting the next day, we would be encountering rough seas. But the captain promised not to abandon us and to take us all the way to Tel Aviv himself. As for the approaching stormy seas, he cautioned us to stay on deck to ride out the bad weather.

The next morning, the waves began to build. On deck, I became afraid of the high waves but became nauseous every time I went below. So I followed the captain's directive and stayed on deck, despite my fear of the water and the violent swaying of the vessel that suddenly seemed so small.

The day after, all passengers and some of the crew were on deck and hanging over the railing for most of the daylight hours, clinging to the balustrade to not fall overboard. The sea didn't relent during the night. Most of the passengers remained on deck.

In the dark, the sea looked even more ominous, and I awaited the moment when the tall waves would swallow us up.

I thought of Paul and anger arose in me like the waves in front of me. He had never warned me or mentioned anything about the rough waters of the Mediterranean. Neither had Nellie or Helene. I was certain they'd left that out purposefully when speaking about journeying to Palestine.

Since I had never been on a ship before, the sea sickness was a new experience for me that I intended never to relive. That night, I promised myself that on no account would I ever set foot on a ship again.

When the sea's anger and thus my own had finally subsided, I noticed a big navy ship far off on the horizon. Others had seen it as well. The crew became very agitated and ordered us below deck. We could feel the engine of the schooner kick into gear and propel us forward. The speed picked up.

When night approached, we were told that we would be landing soon and to be ready for it. We would have to disembark in haste to escape the authorities. Only minutes later, we heard shots and bullets whizzing. The crew screamed at us to lay low, but it was too late for one of the passengers. A bullet had struck a woman. The crew tried in vain to calm the panic that ensued. Only after the captain appeared did people settle down.

In my mind, I cursed Paul once again.

Nellie was oddly quiet. She no longer comforted us as she had done at the beginning of our journey or the first couple of days on the ship. I wondered if she regretted her decision and felt guilty for asking me to come along.

The captain explained to us, the frightened passengers, that the British had discovered us and had shot at our vessel to deter us from landing ashore. He told us that the Royal Navy destroyer we had seen in the distance was on its way and would then escort us to Haifa.

To us, the passengers, it felt as if we were still at war, and as if we were still not wanted. My only comfort would be that we were going straight to Haifa, which hopefully would be the end of my journey. The address that Paul had hastily scribbled down in the infirmary at Auschwitz was in Haifa, after all. So I welcomed the change of course.

When we were finally allowed back on deck, the British destroyer was right next to us. One of our crew members told us that the British would detain us upon arrival in Haifa since we had no proper permission to enter Palestine. I saw the distress I felt in my fellow passengers' faces. We would be prisoners once more.

When the ship anchored in Haifa, we were not taken off the schooner immediately. All passengers were gathered on deck to catch a glimpse of the new land we'd heard so much about and where we weren't welcome. It looked so foreign. An arid land with strange architecture and unfamiliar noises. We stared in wonder at what lay before us but waited anxiously to disembark.

While I couldn't wait to feel steady ground under my feet again, I would also be arrested and thrown in prison from what I understood. Would they keep us locked up or would they send us back? But back where? Most of us had no home or family to return to. And how would Paul, who was perhaps already in Haifa or coming soon, find me then? I would be utterly alone, with no family and friends in Europe.

I carried with me the torn piece of paper on which Paul had hastily scribbled his uncle's address in Haifa. A part of it was missing. I had no idea if I would find him, and if I eventually did, would I be welcome by his family?

What if he wasn't even there?

I had constantly discussed these questions with Nellie who eventually had grown tired of it. No one was waiting for her in Palestine, but she didn't mind that.

After what seemed like hours of waiting, British Navy personnel came on board. I didn't understand any of the directions they were giving us. I didn't speak English or Hebrew, the two languages in which the directives were given. As a child, I had been taught a little Hebrew but not enough to understand what was being said or that would help me adjust and function in a new land where, for the first time in my life, I'd be living among my people, in the land that Helene had longed for. But not understanding and seeing the strange land before me didn't make me feel in any way that I had arrived where I belonged.

Nellie didn't speak any Hebrew either. She had grown up in an assimilated family in Berlin. Her father had been a doctor who'd been baptized into the Lutheran church as a baby. He saw no value in Hebrew lessons for his daughter. The Nazis hadn't cared about his conversion and had still considered him a Jew. Nellie's parents had been deported to the East while she was in hiding. She didn't know where to but like so many of us, had to assume that they had been murdered.

Someone came around to collect our papers. I reluctantly handed mine over to the man in uniform. He scrutinized them and proceeded to ask me and Nellie in perfect German if we had understood any of the instructions. We shook our heads, and he smiled. I didn't return it. He then summarized what had been said and what would happen next. In the end, he told us that we needed to learn Hebrew as quickly as possible and that German wouldn't be of any help in Palestine.

He said goodbye in Hebrew and left with our papers.

I looked toward the land and the seemingly bustling city of Haifa. It was nothing I had expected or imagined. There were no ax-swinging golems on a desert plane that had once invaded my dreams in Chelm. I thought of Bobe and a wave of sadness, as strong as the waves of the Mediterranean, washed over me. I swallowed hard and tried to disperse the dark thoughts. I felt forsaken and desolate like the Palestine I had imagined.

Looking at Nellie, I knew she felt somewhat the same.

After we had stared at the land before us long enough, we went over to the rest of our group to confirm with them what the man in uniform had divulged and to find out if we had surrendered our papers for good. Like everyone else at the displaced person camps, I had received new papers there.

The Nazis had threatened us under punishment of death to always carry our papers with us, only to later take them away at Auschwitz in exchange for a number. Getting new papers after the DP camp had been like retrieving my identity, and becoming human again. And now they had been taken away from me yet again. I frowned at the irony of it all.

Members of our little group confirmed that the British had refused us entry due to our attempt at illegal immigration and that for that reason, we had to stay on board until it was decided what to do with the refugee passengers. In our group was a teacher who'd taught Hebrew in a small school in Poland before the war. Nellie and I would have to rely on him until we learned the language.

When the evening sun was setting, casting a golden-orange glow upon the city, two British army officers came back on board. I was relieved the wait would be over but also anxious. The British seemed to have finally decided what to do with us. The question was what.

We were told to disembark and that since we had entered Palestine illegally, we would be detained. Immediately, protests mounted all around us. When our captain got arrested, a woman screamed. Panic broke out, and people started pushing. I could feel dread beginning to engulf me.

Our group huddled together, but one by one we were pulled off the schooner and moved onto an open-bed truck that would take us to a detention camp.

When I sat on the truck, I thought of Hershel who had died in a Gestapo prison only days after our arrest. I looked around and into the faces of the other detainees. The shock and dismay in everyone's face looked all too familiar. Once more, we would be carted off to a camp.

The irony made me chuckle.

Nellie stared at me with furrowed brows, and I scolded myself. Clearing my throat, I looked at the ground. Regret was all I felt. Regret that I'd left the DP camp and followed Nellie, and regret and guilt that I'd chosen Paul over Georg and Clara.

I wished Paul had never given me his uncle's address and made me promise to come to Palestine. Why did I go to the end of the world for him? Did Paul not know that we Jews were not wanted anywhere?

———

After a half an hour's ride on the truck, we arrived at a camp called Atlit which was located just to the south of Haifa. The barbed wire and watchtowers told us that this was a concentration camp. So the Nazis hadn't been the only ones with these types of camps, Nellie noted sarcastically.

We were ushered off the trucks and told to set our suitcases aside and line up, men and women separately. A guard came and barked orders. We pleaded with the teacher in our group to translate, but he only stared ahead, his lips tight. He was trembling and a pool of liquid formed around his feet.

I panicked and fell out of line. A guard snapped at me. A woman behind me pulled me back. "Stay calm," she hissed. From the back of the line, a man yelled, "They are taking us to the disinfection barracks." Panic broke out all around me. Women were screaming, and I'd never before heard the guttural sounds the men made. I kneaded my hands to prevent them from trembling.

It took the guards several minutes to calm us down and to have everyone in line again. No one had been beaten or shot. That did reassure us a little.

My line started moving, and once again, we were marching. And we were exceptionally good at it.

On our way to the disinfection barracks, I scanned my surroundings for chimneys. I was glad to see none. When we arrived, a great silence had fallen on our group of women. We were ushered in calmly and told to undress to disinfect. None of us spoke. Every movement I made during undressing was as consciously done as taking my last breath.

The showers were indeed just showers, but I went through the whole process numbly. Last time, my sisters and I had clung to each other. But they were gone, and I was experienced.

Nellie, who had been in hiding for most of the war before joining partisans in the East, had never had the experience, but she had heard of the showers and gas chambers. I saw her trembling next to me and put my arm around her shoulders. "These are just showers, trust me," I said with put on light-heartedness, trying to reassure her and myself. I hoped and prayed I was right.

The showers were indeed just showers, and we sighed in collective relief. Afterwards, we were handed new clothing. To all of our great relief again, it was civilian clothing, not prisoners' uniforms. Some of the women smiled when they were handed the fresh new clothes.

Once we had changed, we were allowed to retrieve our suitcases and were led to our accommodations.

We were housed in barracks, wooden structures with decent cot beds awaiting us inside. I had no idea how long we would be detained but when I sank down on the bed, I sighed in relief.

Nellie chose the one next to me and immediately lay down to fall asleep only a couple of minutes later. The exhaustion from the journey started to settle over me as well. I lay down, too, and fell into a deep sleep that didn't offer any dreams.

Weeks went by in Atlit. We spent our days reading, walking around our side of the camp, singing songs from home, and learning Hebrew and Zionist songs. Our Hebrew teacher was a German Jew also from Berlin called Rachel. Nellie instantly took to her. They exchanged childhood stories and reminisced about places in Berlin they were both familiar with.

Rachel had fled Germany and come to Palestine ten years ago without speaking any Hebrew herself. She understood our plight and tried to teach us the language as quickly as possible.

The Hebrew lessons were the highlight of our day, breaking up the monotony of camp life. One day ran into another. A great boredom began to settle over us. We were told it could be months until our release.

One evening, when the searing summer sun had made way for an exceptionally starry night, we sat in a circle on the struggling grass outside our barracks and went around the circle to share about our life before and during the war. We had never talked much about the war or Auschwitz and only rarely did we speak about our families. It was all still too painful and most of us had no words to express what we had seen and lost.

When it was my turn to share, I simply stated that I was a seamstress.

Nellie looked at me in shock. "You are?" she asked.

I nodded and looked at the ground. I regretted not saying that I was a teacher instantly. Talking about sewing and giving any more detail would inevitably lead me to speak about my family. And I just couldn't yet.

A couple of women asked questions which I answered tersely and vaguely.

When the next woman shared details about her life, my thoughts wandered to my Minerva. I hadn't thought about it or sewing since I'd left Auschwitz. I looked at my hands and examined my fingers resting in my lap. The fabric of my skirt felt rough against my palms.

After my Hebrew class the next day, I asked Rachel if she could teach me a few additional words and if she could look over a dialogue I had prepared. She pulled me with her to the shady side of the barracks and we sat down. When she was reading through my dialogue, which I had written down with some effort, she raised her eyebrows but didn't comment on its content. She made a few suggestions and crossed out a couple of words only to write the correct terms above them.

The next morning, I went to the administrative building and asked in my minimal and halting Hebrew if they had a sewing machine I could use. The woman at the front desk asked me what I needed it for. "To sew," I told her incredulously.

It turned out that detainees at a British concentration camp were not allowed to work or perform any activities that could be construed as work. I assured them that it was not to work but rather to pass the time and keep my skills sharp. It had been over a year and a half since I'd last sat in front of a sewing machine.

I was promised that the matter would be brought before the commander.

Two days later, I was called to the administrative building. When I entered, my eye immediately caught the shiny black machine that was sitting on a side table. I went over to it and ran my hand across the golden lettering. A Minerva. I swallowed hard and tried to suppress the tears that threatened to well up.

Someone cleared their throat behind me, and I quickly pulled my hand back and turned around to face the woman I'd spoken to a couple of days earlier.

"You may come here daily. To sew. Right here. You're not allowed to take it with you to your housing," the clerk said.

"Thank you," I said and moved toward the machine.

"I will bring you some fabric and yarn tomorrow," she added, her voice kind. I smiled and nodded. "Come back tomorrow afternoon."

I left the administration building with a spring in my steps. Tomorrow would be a new day. Tomorrow would be a new beginning or a return to my beginning.

———

The camp became bearable. Between my Hebrew lessons in the morning and sewing in the afternoon, time passed by. One day, after months in Atlit, the commander awaited me when I walked into the administrative building.

"How would you like to own a machine like this?" he asked me. My Hebrew was getting pretty fluent after so much consistent study, and I understood him despite his British accent. I was taken aback by his question and seeing him waiting for me. He'd never paid any attention to me in the past when I had passed him. "I once owned a machine just like that one, sir," I said, pointing at the Minerva.

"It's yours then. You will need it." At my puzzled look, he added, "Someone has offered to employ you. You have permission to reside and work in Palestine. You're being released tomorrow." I looked from him to the clerk, who gave me a wink.

I gaped at them for a moment before snapping my jaw shut and offering a quick "thank you," which was completely insufficient.

He nodded and went to his office.

I stood there until the clerk called me over. "We better get started on your paperwork," she said with a smile. "And I'm sure you have many questions."

"I do." My mind was racing. "Who is my employer?"

The clerk winked at me again. "My cousin is a tailor in Haifa, and he needs help. You seemed to be very capable. So I told him about you."

"Thank you," was all I brought out. I would be forever grateful to that kind woman. And I could finally search for Paul's uncle in Haifa, who would likely know of his whereabouts. Or maybe ... Paul would be there to finally embrace me.

But then I thought of Nellie. I would leave her behind.

I returned to the barracks feeling guilty that I would abandon her. But when I arrived, she stood over her cot, packing. I looked at her with raised eyebrows. When she saw me, she smiled. "I'm getting released tomorrow," she said carefully as if the news would hurt me.

"You are?" I stepped up to her cot and started to help her pack.

The genuine joy in my voice must have been encouraging because she added, "They need teachers. Sara, they will need you, too."

I grinned at her. "Guess what, I'll be leaving tomorrow, too." She looked dumbfounded but then broke into the biggest smile I'd ever seen on her. "The clerk got me a job as a seamstress in Haifa."

"How wonderful!" She hugged me. But when she let go, she looked sad. "I'll be teaching in Tel Aviv."

"Do not worry. We'll visit each other," I said to reassure her. I gave her the name and address of the seamstress I'd be working for in Haifa. In return, she promised to write.

We helped each other pack and promised to visit whenever we could.

The next morning, we stepped outside the camp and said our goodbyes. In addition to my suitcase, I lugged along the Minerva.

After a week in Haifa, I finally found the courage again to look at the scribbled note Paul had given me. The penciling had almost entirely vanished and a piece of the address was missing but luckily, the street name was still decipherable. In my hand, it felt like an old relic from a time that seemed so long ago. A relic from a world that I sometimes caught myself questioning if it had truly existed. Without its existence, I was sure I'd believe the moment in which Paul had come to my bedside and had pressed the paper in my hand never happened. It was a moment steeped in haziness. But the note in my hand was real, and Paul had been real.

So, one early Friday afternoon after work, I ventured in the direction of the harbor where I was told I'd find the street. The roads around the harbor were busy and loud. I grew impatient and stopped to ask for directions. A kind old woman pointed into a side street. A hundred meters ahead, I spotted the awning of a cafe. Tables with chairs lined that part of the street. I swallowed and walked toward it, holding the note more tightly.

Taking a deep breath, I stepped inside the café. In my dreams, I'd always run into Paul's arms in front of it. But Paul wasn't there, and I was anxious to find out if I was in the right place.

The cafe looked warm and welcoming inside. Dark wood paneled the walls. It almost looked like the coffeehouses in Vienna. It was almost completely empty inside. Most customers were seated at the tables outside. I took a seat at one of the empty tables by the door and waited. A young woman came toward me shortly after, greeting me with a smile.

"What can I bring you?" she asked.

"Just a coffee, please." I looked up at her and smiled. "Could you tell me if Albert is here today?" I added, almost holding my breath.

"He'll be back in half an hour," she said and left. So, I was in the right place. And half an hour wasn't too long of a wait, but I also knew that my anxiety would only increase with each passing minute.

I saw some magazines and newspapers on a counter nearby and went to grab one. I had to pass the time as quickly as I could and distract myself. I looked through the selection and spotted the *Israel-Nachrichten*, a German-speaking newspaper I'd consistently read in the camp. While it hadn't taught me any Hebrew, I'd learned a lot about the culture, society, and politics in Palestine. But I put it aside and took up a copy of the *Palestine Post* instead. My Hebrew was solid enough that I could read the local newspapers, and I was proud to speak it near-fluently.

Taking tiny sips of my coffee, I immersed myself in it in an attempt to take my mind off the wait.

I didn't even notice when Uncle Albert arrived. The waitress came over to let me know that he was back. I asked her to speak to him.

A couple of minutes later, a tall man with a solid build stood in front of me. He reminded me of Paul. He was perhaps in his late fifties, or early sixties, but he was unmistakably related to Paul. "You asked to speak to me?"

I cleared my throat and stood up. The newspaper glided to the floor.

"No need to get up," he said. "I'm not the mayor of Haifa." He looked amused.

I stretched out my hand, and he took it. "I'm Sara."

"Sara ..." The blood drained from Uncle Albert's tanned face. "You're here." I nodded but couldn't bring out a word. "I was told you would come. Paul managed to get word to me from—" he struggled for the word. "Auschwitz? Yes, that's the place." He nodded to himself.

"He wrote to you?" I wondered how Paul had managed to send out a letter, but then I remembered the chaos of the day when he'd come to tell me goodbye. He must have managed then. But I also knew Paul had had some good connections in the camp. "Paul told me to come to Haifa and seek you out," I said hesitantly. I held out the scribbled note as evidence.

He looked at it for a moment. He didn't take it but instead pulled me into a hug.

"I'm glad you made it, Sara." He let go of me and looked at me carefully, biting his lower lip. "But ... Paul isn't here. He hasn't arrived yet." I could tell he was trying to hide his concern. I did not attempt to hide my disappointment. "Sit back down, Sara. Please," Uncle Albert said. Perhaps he thought I would faint at the news.

I retook my seat, and he claimed a chair across from me. "Paul told me to come here. To meet him here." Uncle Albert nodded but let me continue. "He said to wait for him in Haifa." Tears welled up in me. "I'd like to come here every day and wait for him. If you'll allow it?"

"Of course." He looked at me intently. "We heard the reports coming out of Europe. Was it really as bad as they say?" He must have noticed my furrowed brows and puzzled look. "But let's not talk about that now. Let's just be glad the war is over. I will close up soon for Shabbat. You must join us for dinner. The family is there and will want to meet you."

I swallowed. I didn't feel like meeting Paul's family tonight. The disappointment that Paul wasn't here was too great. And I would perhaps have to share things I wasn't ready to talk about.

But as I studied Uncle Albert's friendly face, there was no way I was able to say no to that man.

CHAPTER 12

1947

U ncle Albert stepped outside with my coffee. I caught a whiff of the fresh brew that now overshadowed the fishy smell of the harbor. He placed the coffee in front of me with a smile and moved on to the next table. The comfort of the café together with Uncle Albert's presence made me feel almost content but then, every time I looked into those deep brown eyes, so dark you couldn't make out the pupil, and when I explored the freckles of his skin, I felt that little stab to the heart that would take my breath away. How much he looked like Paul. But Uncle Albert was stockier, and his hair was entirely white.

I took a sip of the hot liquid and leaned back in my chair. How long had it been? How long had I been coming there? Every evening after work. For months. Still no word. I closed my eyes and held my face toward the dying sun.

When I opened them, there he was again. He must have just sat down because I'd not seen him earlier. As always, he wore a white shirt and gray trousers, the kind Father had tailored so skillfully and worn himself for leisure.

The café patron seemed a few years older than me, perhaps my brother Georg's age. He smoked a couple of cigarettes a day and had a couple of coffees each visit. The same ritual. His brown hair hung in curls into his face, and he had a slim stature that reminded me of Paul.

He'd been coming for weeks. I saw him every evening without fail. He never said a word to anyone other than Uncle Albert, never stared, but last week, I'd caught his eyes and held his gaze for a moment. He'd smiled, and I'd looked away. I'd felt uncomfortable and had left a couple of minutes later.

A few weeks later, in early June, on one of those evenings when the oppressive heat in Haifa brought all its citizens out of their homes, I sat as usual at my table sipping my coffee and thumbing lazily through a magazine. The big umbrella gave me just enough shade to make it bearable to sit outside in the evening sun.

I had just ordered another coffee when the stranger appeared. I had made it a point of completely ignoring him and not looking in his direction to avoid getting caught in his gaze.

He didn't approach his usual table but sat down at the one to the right of me. He wore the same shirt and trousers as always, but his sleeves were rolled up to combat the heat.

As he sat down, I uncomfortably shifted in my seat, but my eye caught something. I saw what was unmistakably a tattoo of numbers on his forearm.

It took all my willpower not to stare. I didn't need to. The image of numbers burnt into the flesh of a forearm was irrevocably imprinted on my mind's eye.

The magazine in my hands became my sole focus. I stared at the images and text on the pages so hard, they started to blur, and I couldn't comprehend what I stared at. My mind raced, images swimming in and out of it.

A few minutes later, Uncle Albert came out with another coffee for me, but today he took a seat across from me. I was once more grateful for his presence and for interrupting my thoughts.

I put the magazine down and smiled at him, but I couldn't read his expression. It was cold and stern. My face fell. "What's wrong?"

He pulled out a paper from his shirt pocket, unfolded it, and pushed it toward me. I could only stare at it. My hands rested in my lap, holding on tightly to each other. I looked up at him and back at the paper. My mind was racing. My throat was thickening. I tried to focus on my breath as I had done so many times, but my breathing became rapid regardless.

I reached for the paper with a trembling hand, but Uncle Albert grabbed my whole arm, holding it tightly. "I think you knew already," he said.

I pulled my arm away. "How—" I choked out. He looked at me, confused. "How did he die?" I added.

Uncle Albert leaned back slowly. "There were usually two ways how people died on these horrible death marches. They either keeled over from exhaustion or they were shot because they couldn't keep up."

I shook my head, not at Uncle Albert but to disburse the images in my head. I knew that the thought of me was, what had made Paul hang on. Shot? I got up. "I need to go."

Uncle Albert stood with me. He reached for the paper, but I was quicker. I crunched it in my hand and took it with me.

———

I wasn't sure why I was still coming to the café every evening, but it had been my routine and refuge for so long. And I felt close to Paul there. I knew he was gone and that there was no hope of ever being able to look into those dark eyes again. But being there, at Uncle Albert's café, gave me comfort. And I didn't have to be anywhere else or with anyone else.

Georg had written to me and urged me again to join him, his family, and Clara, whom he had already brought to America. He had gotten married and had two young boys. My only family. The Georg in the pictures he had sent looked so much like Father. I longed to be with him, his family, and Clara, the only sister I had left and who I missed so much. But the thought of Clara also brought pain.

Would being in her presence, too? Would the guilt I felt over refusing to send Ruth with her ever cease? *Can you forgive me, little Ruth?* I swallowed hard and took a sip of my coffee as if I could wash down the guilt with Uncle Albert's brew, then stared into it as if it could offer me guidance. But it had none.

It was time to let go. Of the waiting at the café. Of hope for Paul. He was gone. He had never come as he'd promised. I needed to join Georg and Clara in America.

I pulled out a book from my purse, determined to seriously start planning my move to America, to make plans for the future, to leave Haifa, the café, and Uncle Albert, to begin a new life and leave it all behind. Once and for all. I needed to.

But not until tomorrow.

I would sit there and wait for Paul. One last time. To truly bid him farewell in my own little way. I swallowed hard and turned my attention to the book.

"My name is Claude." His French accent was very strong. I looked up from my book and froze. The stranger was talking to me? Why? What did he want? "May I sit?" he added.

I nodded reluctantly. Uncle Albert came with another cup of coffee but to my surprise, he put it in front of Claude. Uncle Albert shot me a quick smile before he left.

"I saw your tattoo one day," I blurted out and regretted it immediately. He looked at me in surprise.

"You have one, too, I noticed," he said. I ran my thumb over the numbers. "But what is your name?" he asked.

"Sara."

He then told me his whole story. I told him I didn't want to hear it, but he continued relentlessly. He spoke so freely about it, something I'd never been able to do. Especially not to a stranger.

His account of his time in Auschwitz was not much different from mine, but then again, so much different from mine.

When he spoke of the death march to Dachau in the cruel winter of 1945, I held up my hand. "You were on that march?" I leaned forward. I suddenly wanted to know every detail of his story.

With the Soviet army approaching, the SS had marched thousands of Auschwitz prisoners toward the interior of the Reich. Few had made it from what I'd learned. I'd been told that Paul had been sent on the one to Dachau. In my feverish state, I'd only half registered the news back then.

But there was no way that Claude knew Paul, right? Could they have been on the same death march?

For a moment, I played with the thought of asking him, but his story had already exhausted me too much. He needed to finish so I could leave.

"Yes, I was on that march. We left Auschwitz some time in mid-January, I think it was," he said, pulling out a cigarette. He offered me one, but I shook my head. I needed him to continue. It all seemed like a hundred years ago, another lifetime ago. And that's how I liked it.

Claude stopped and leaned back, eyeing me. Then his eyes darkened. "Most of us were too weak to make that journey, you know." The intensity in his eyes made me shift in my seat. "Two days after we left Auschwitz, we rose up against them. Against the SS guards who were driving us on. They shot anyone who couldn't keep up. If you ended up in the back of the column, you'd be shot.

"We helped each other as best as we could, but we were all so exhausted. The sides of the road were littered with corpses, prisoners who had been shot for being too slow or too weak to go on. Some simply fell down and never got up. So about fifty of us revolted. We attacked them and tried to take their guns. We resisted, Sara. You should have seen their faces. The panic in their eyes. But so many of us were shot in that fight. Too many.

"I only survived because my friend shoved me into a ditch. They shot him. He gave his life for me that day." He fell silent and his eyes grew even darker. He looked up at me again. "Paul was the one who shoved me into that ditch. After the SS had run off with the rest of the prisoners, I climbed out of the ravine and found Paul still breathing." He paused for a moment. "I watched my friend die."

Paul ...

My head spun and my vision blurred. I tried to steady my breath. He had given his life for the man in front of me. He had sacrificed our life together for another. I swallowed hard. The leaden silence that followed was heavier than the oppressive heat hanging over Haifa.

Claude didn't speak for a long while. He let me be, and I was grateful for it. My mind raced as fast as my heart, and I tried in vain to push away the images that I'd been able to keep at bay for almost two years.

When the sun dipped behind the buildings, Claude took out another cigarette and continued his account.

He told me that Paul and he had been friends since they'd worked in *Kanada* together and that Paul had shared our story, how we met, had fallen in love, and tried to help each other survive. Paul had never mentioned Claude to me but had told him everything about me, my family, all the details about my life I didn't want a stranger to know. Then with his dying breath, Paul had told Claude about his promise to me, to meet me at Uncle Albert's café in Haifa after the war. That I would wait for him there or he for me.

And he'd made Claude promise to go in his stead. To find me, to tell me that he was so very sorry he couldn't make it himself. And that he loved me.

Claude halted the flow of his words when I started sobbing. I lost all control. There in the café, in front of a stranger named Claude and onlookers. He sat silently and let me weep.

I wept for Paul, for the life we would never spend together, for the hope that Claude had completely crushed with his story and his presence. I was supposed to cry tears of happiness in the café one day upon seeing Paul come down the street and sit across from me. Us sipping coffee together and planning our lives together.

Claude's hand rested on my arm. I pulled away. He was a stranger.

A stranger Paul had given his life for.

"I know this must have been hard to hear," Claude said, interrupting my grief. "But I also know that one day, you will appreciate that you learned what happened to him. I never learned what happened to my parents. So many of us don't know what exactly happened to our families."

"I'm sorry about your parents," I said, barely audible.

"They were rounded up in Paris with many other foreign Jews in July of 1942 and then held in a stadium."

"They weren't French?" I asked.

"No, my parents were originally from Poland. I grew up speaking Yiddish."

"What happened to your parents?" I realized the stupidity of my question. "I'm sorry," I mumbled quickly.

Claude looked at me, his face a mixture of pain and guilt. I lowered my head, ashamed of how cold I'd been to the man who had gone out of his way to make sure he delivered Paul's message to me. To make sure *I* knew what had happened.

"I learned that they were sent to some transit camp outside the city shortly after," Claude said, interrupting my thoughts. "I don't know anything else, but I wish I did." He paused and eyed his pack of cigarettes on the table but chose not to take one yet. "I wish I had been there with them. I *should* have been there with them," he said, his face grim. "I'll never forgive myself for abandoning them."

Now it was me who reached out and touched his arm. He looked up at me and mustered a faint smile.

"You couldn't have done anything for them," I said.

"I could have at least been with them, Sara," he said. "But I was fighting with the résistance. As their only child, I should have been there for them. Stayed with them."

Only then did I notice that he'd placed his hand on mine. He seemed to realize it at the same moment and withdrew. He mumbled an apology and sat back. "Let me walk you home?"

"That would be nice." I was surprised by my words, but how could I refuse him? He needed company as much as I did, and he'd given me closure, something all of us, the survivors, yearned for.

We left the cafe and walked leisurely down the street toward the harbor with me leading the way.

"So, you live down by the harbor, too, I see. Makes for a quick getaway, doesn't it?" He mused.

"Yes, many of the survivors live there, don't they," I said.

We walked on in silence for a little bit, but then Claude told me about his childhood in Paris, the beautiful architecture, the parks, the corner cafes, and the delicious foods. I listened with wide eyes and even caught myself smiling at the stories he shared. He was a wonderful storyteller.

In the end, I found myself sharing about the happy parts of my own childhood. I talked about my parents and my sisters, my summers in Chelm with Bobe and Zayde, and my love for sewing. I hadn't talked about my family and my happy memories of them in such a long time. It felt good to share about them and that time of my life. It was healing, and I was surprised that my heart didn't hurt as much as I thought it would by talking about them.

The smell of the sea and fish grew stronger as we approached the alley where I lived. When we arrived at the building where I rented a room in the flat of an old widow, I thanked him for walking me home. He nodded and smiled at me. "If you ever feel like coffee and would like someone to talk to, I'm your man."

CHAPTER 13

SPRING 1948

C laude and I saw each other almost every evening, and I was glad for it. He became my friend. I knew he was hoping for more, but I was still grieving Paul.

On Wednesdays, we went to Uncle Albert's café together, to sit, talk, have coffee, and relax together after work. We both looked forward to Wednesdays. We felt close to Paul at the cafe, and this was our way of including him.

When we sat outside at the café in the evening sun, Claude happily shared with me the stories he was working on and swore me to secrecy with a twinkle of his eye not to share them with anyone before their publication. He'd found work with The Palestine Post. He'd studied journalism in Paris before the war. I was embarrassed by the little schooling I had received in comparison, but I didn't tell him how I felt about that.

On other days, we took long walks by the sea and looked toward Europe. We missed home, but we both knew, that the home we'd known, no longer existed.

One evening, in early spring, there was an increased commotion in the harbor and an increased presence of British troops. I asked Claude about it. His face immediately grew dark. "The British are leaving, Sara. War is coming."

I gaped at him. He placed the palm of his hand on my cheek, and I leaned into it, for comfort and reassurance. "I don't want to see another war," I said. "I never want to see war again." Without a word, he drew me in and hugged me tightly. The faint smell of aftershave and cigarettes oddly made me feel at home. I breathed in deeply. He let go of me but not without first kissing my hair.

Occasionally, Claude surprised me with flowers that brightened the small room I rented. Waking up to the flowers and their fragrance lifted my spirits in the morning and carried me for the rest of the day. I soon realized that I'd begun to think of Claude each morning right when I woke up. Although I enjoyed my work and appreciated the kindness of the woman who employed me, I couldn't wait for the daylight to wane so I could see Claude.

I was growing quite fond of him.

Eventually, Uncle Albert invited Claude to Shabbat dinner as well. I was happy to take him along, and Claude was glad to no longer eat alone on the holy day. Like many of the survivors, we had been adopted by family who were not of our blood, yet we were bonded together by loss.

Uncle Albert's grandchildren especially took to Claude. They were happy to have an uncle who told them entertaining stories and played soccer with them in the beautiful garden at the back of Uncle Albert's house where palm trees and the most fragrant flowers grew on trees and bushes I'd never seen before. I loved watching Claude become so playful and light-hearted. I doubted I could ever feel completely at ease around children again, like he did, though. The heaviness of the deaths of Alice's girls still clung to me.

One evening, when Claude had promised to pick me up from work, he didn't come. I waited in front of the little tailoring shop where I worked. I waited until the shadow of Mount Carmel dipped the city around me into darkness. I ignored the disappointment and worries in my gut and made my way home, but I walked purposefully slow in case Claude was just late and tried to catch up with me. Every few steps, I looked over my shoulder to see if he was coming. But he wasn't.

When I arrived home, I looked at the wilting flowers and realized that I missed him—that I loved him. That I could no longer be without him. That I wanted to see him every day for the rest of my life. But why had he not come and picked me up from work as he had promised? I tried to push my worries aside but found little sleep that night.

The sun had not even risen when there was a knock on the door. I must have dozed off after all because I woke up, completely disoriented. Dazed, I climbed out of bed and opened the door to my little room. Outside stood the widow with whom I lived—and Claude.

His shirt was torn and his hair was disheveled. A smudge of blood grazed his cheek. "Sara, pack your things. We will need to go to Uncle Albert's."

I looked from him to the widow. The kind old woman's face showed sadness and resignation. "You need to go where it's safer, dear," she said.

"Why? What is happening? And what about you?" There had been the occasional shots fired and reports of skirmishes in the city between Arabs and Jews but nothing that would warrant getting up in the middle of the night and fleeing. And we couldn't just leave the old widow alone.

Claude entered my room and started packing my things. I just stared at him as an all too familiar numbness crept in, a numbness I thought I'd never feel again. "Sara, please get dressed," he said gently.

"What about her?" I pointed at the door, but the old widow was no longer standing there.

"She's leaving, too. Please get dressed. Now," he said more firmly.

I grabbed a skirt and blouse and went to the washroom to get changed.

When I returned, he was done stuffing my belongings in my suitcase.

"What happened, Claude? I was so worried about you last night. When you didn't come."

He looked at me, his face unreadable. "There was an ambush. I was sent there by the paper to find out what had happened. To report on it. And I got caught in the middle."

His words scared me. I could tell he downplayed what had happened. His torn shirt and the crusted-over cut on his cheek told a different story. He grabbed my hand and pulled me out of the room with him, carrying my suitcase in the other hand.

On my way out, I stole a last glance at the room I'd called home since my release from the camp and arrival in Haifa. The wilted flowers looked as if the room's inhabitant had left a while ago.

On our way to Uncle Albert's home, Claude weaved in and out of dark alleys. We crept toward our destination in the shadows of houses and under the cloak of the night. In the distance, gunfire echoed.

When we arrived at Uncle Albert's home, we went around the back where he greeted us and quickly ushered us in. Claude and he discussed how the British were almost completely gone and that a battle for Haifa would soon commence. Arab and Jewish militias were already fighting each other, and the confrontations were not without attacks on civilians, looting, and other violence. Claude informed Uncle Albert that he'd heard that martial law would be declared tomorrow.

He turned to me. "Sara, do you want to leave? With me?"

Leave? Haifa? Palestine? Uncle Albert? And where to?

Claude came over to me and took both of my hands in his. "I don't want to see another war. And I know you don't want to, either. Let's leave. Together." He paused and let go of my hands, only to take my face in his. "Will you marry me, Sara?" I stared at him in utter disbelief.

My eye caught Uncle Albert, who was standing behind Claude. A big grin framed his face and he nodded vigorously.

"I don't know ... what to say ..."

"Say yes. I love you, Sara. Do you love me?"

I looked into his dark eyes, and I had to be honest with myself. And him. "I do."

"Then marry me, Sara. Say yes." He embraced me. My head spun, so I buried my face in his shoulder and breathed in deeply. I thought of Paul. It had become less and less painful to think about him, and I knew he would approve. After all, he'd sent Claude to me.

"Yes," I whispered. He buried his face in my hair and gently kissed it.

Big arms enveloped us. Uncle Albert had joined our embrace. I laughed heartily at his excitement. He'd become a father to me.

"As soon as the sun is up, I will seek out the rabbi and make the arrangements," Uncle Albert said, squeezing us tightly.

When we let go of each other, I said, "We'll go to America. Georg will finally get his wish." While it saddened me to leave my newfound family that had been so welcoming and had taken us in, it was finally time to reunite with mine.

Claude and I were married two days later. It was a small wedding. Like many other survivors' weddings, we had no parents, grandparents, or siblings in attendance, but we had Paul's family who had become our own.

Saying goodbye and leaving them only a few days later was difficult. We would miss them and hoped that they'd stay safe. But war was coming, and we had to go where it could not reach us. Claude and I got on a ship, despite the promise I'd made to myself to never do so again, and made our way to America.

EPILOGUE
2019

I open my eyes. My granddaughter is holding my hand, her thumb caressing my arm. She stops short of the numbers on my forearm as if touching them would hurt me.

The oxygen pump to the side of my bed is pulsing with constant fervor. The door opens, and Paul comes in, his face solemn. He lost his father a few years ago and now it is my time. At last.

I'm patting my granddaughter's hand and whisper: "Ruth, take care of your father, will you?" She nods. Her eyes well and she sniffs back tears. "And don't forget to say the *Kaddish* for me, dear."

"Of course I will, Oma. We all will. Like you taught us. For all of you."

I relax back on my pillow and breathe in the oxygen, the scent of the mask's silicone an odd comfort. I try to ignore the pain in my chest. No more pacemakers.

It is time to let go.

GLOSSARY

Anweiser: [German] instructor

Appell: [German] roll call

Appellplatz: [German] square in concentration and extermination camps where roll calls and selections were held

Kaddish: [Aramaic] the prayer of mourners in Judaism

Kanada: [German] warehouses at Auschwitz-Birkenau that stored valuables and confiscated possessions of the victims

Kapo: [German] a camp inmate selected by the SS to oversee other prisoners on work details

Sonderkommando: [German] groups of camp prisoners forced to perform various tasks in the gas chambers and crematoria

Yahrzeit: [Yiddish] the anniversary of a loved one's death

ABOUT THE AUTHOR

C. K. McAdam writes historical fiction and women's fiction. She holds a Ph.D. in Interdisciplinary Humanities and teaches college. Together with her family, she resides in Texas but hails originally from Germany where she grew up. In her free time, she loves to travel, hike, read historical fiction, play pickleball, spend time with her family, and go on walks with her corgi Merlin.

Subscribe to the author's newsletter by visiting **www.mcadambooks.com** for more info, news, and updates. Connect with the author on social media and don't hesitate to leave reviews. Every author appreciates them very much.

amazon.com/author/ckmcadam

instagram.com/ckmcadam

facebook.com/ckmcadam

twitter.com/CK_McAdam

ALSO BY

C. K. McAdam

NO MAN'S LAND

THE POET'S DAUGHTER (Summer 2024)

Acknowledgements

While most of the characters in this novel are fictitious, Sara's story was inspired by true events. Hedwig Höss, wife to Auschwitz-Birkenau commander Rudolf Höss, did indeed run a fashion salon in the infamous Nazi extermination camp, using skilled seamstress prisoners to do her bidding. These women were ordered to create beautiful fashion for the wives of SS guards, officers, and Nazi bigwigs.

I want to acknowledge several sources I consulted in my research for this novel, among them the archives of the United States Holocaust Memorial Museum, the Yad Vashem World Holocaust Remembrance Center, the Jewish Virtual Library, the Mahn- und Gedenkstätte Ravensbrück, and the Memorial and Museum Auschwitz-Birkenau as well as Lucy Adlington's book *The Dressmakers of Auschwitz*, Sarah Helm's *If This Is a Woman: Hitler's Concentration Camp for Women*, and Israel Gutman's and Michael Berenbaum's *Anatomy of the Auschwitz Death Camp*.

Special thanks go to my alpha and beta readers whose support and enthusiasm for my writing and helpful suggestions for this novel were invaluable and are always appreciated.

And of course, a big thank you to my readers, fans, and superfans, and all the lovely bookclubs for loving the stories I have to tell and for patiently waiting for my next release.

And while it will seem cliche, I need and want to thank my family and friends for their encouragement, for believing in me, and for supporting my journey as an author. Among other things, it is their encouragement that keeps me writing.

My heartfelt appreciation and love also to my girls, my little women, who I have told since they were little, that sisters are forever. They inspired some character traits in Sara and her sisters. Speaking of sisters ... Everyone needs one. My own sister who I don't deserve is a great example of motherhood and a wonderful friend to me.

Last but not least, I want to thank my husband who comes from a country of storytellers and is one himself. He's my greatest supporter, one of my alpha readers, and my superfan. Without his support, encouragement, advice, and guidance, I wouldn't be the author I am.

Made in the USA
Columbia, SC
24 May 2024

36148225R00148